OFF THE ROAD

by Nina Bawden

PUFFIN BOOKS

PUFFIN BOOKS
Published by the Penguin Group
Penguin Putnam Books for Young Readers,
345 Hudson Street, New York, New York 10014, U.S.A.
Penguin Books Ltd, 27 Wrights Lane, London W8 5TZ, England
Penguin Books Australia Ltd, Ringwood, Victoria, Australia
Penguin Books Canada Ltd, 10 Alcorn Avenue, Toronto, Ontario, Canada M4V 3B2
Penguin Books (N.Z.) Ltd, 182-190 Wairau Road, Auckland 10, New Zealand

Penguin Books Ltd, Registered Offices: Harmondsworth, Middlesex, England

First published in the United States of America by Houghton Mifflin Company, 1998
Published by Puffin Books,
a division of Penguin Putnam Books for Young Readers, 2001

1 3 5 7 9 10 8 6 4 2

LIBRARY OF CONGRESS CATALOGING-IN-PUBLICATION DATA
Bawden, Nina, date
Off the road / Nina Bawden.
p. cm.
Summary: In 2040, eleven-year-old Tom follows his grandfather
through the Wall and into the forbidden Wild, where they
seek to find his grandfather's boyhood home.
ISBN 0-14-131100-2
[1. Science Fiction. 2. Grandfathers—Fiction.] I. Title.
PZ7.B33 Of 2001 [Fic]—dc21 00-062669

Printed in the United States of America

For Jack Bawden-Bouché,
the first of the new generation.

OFF
THE
ROAD

Chapter 1

"Now or never . . ."

They were halfway to the Memory Theme Park when Gandy escaped.

Not that Tom thought "escaped" to begin with. More like "flipped his lid." "Lost his marbles."

They had stopped at the Electricity Supply Station to recharge the car and Gandy had gone to the Men's to pee. "Pump ship," was what he called it, an expression Tom had thought brilliantly funny when he had been younger. Now he was eleven, it just seemed the sort of silly euphemism that gave Oldies a bad name.

All the same, thinking about it made him want to go too. As he sloped off, his father looked up from checking the Electricity Monitor and said, unexpectedly sharply, "Leave Gandy alone, Tom."

And his mother, whose name was Penny, added, "It's not far to the next Station, darling."

This made no sense to Tom. They were always on at him not to leave it until he was bursting. He said, indignantly, "I can't *wait*—" and put on a spurt to make it convincing.

He entered the Men's at a trot. It was empty. There was no one at the urinals and all the stall doors were open. He said, "Gandy?" and his voice echoed back from the cold tiles.

Gandy. Gandy—*Gandhi* . . .

He remembered how his grandfather had disliked being called Gandhi. Tom had started calling him Gandy when he was a little boy and couldn't get his tongue around Grandad. Later on, Penny said it should be spelled *Gandhi,* explaining that this was a famous historical person way, way back in the last century, who had been an Indian gentleman and a famous cricketer.

Gandy had exploded. "For Heaven's sake, girl, that is utter rubbish. Gandhi was a saint, not a cricketer! Not many cricketers are saints. Certainly not revolutionary saints!"

But he had sounded tired, rather than angry. He had said, at once, "Sorry, Pen. Not your fault. They'd stopped teaching any sort of history by the time you went to school." Then he had tweaked Tom's ear. "Call me what you like, lad. Gandy.

Grandad. Grandfather. James. Mr. Jacobs. Whatever. If I'm this side of the grave, I'll do my best to answer."

Standing in the empty Men's, Tom said, "Grandad?"

There was a draft coming from somewhere, a puff of cool air. There was a black door at the far end of the Men's. It said NO EXIT, in yellow paint, but it stood a little ajar. Tom pushed it open and found himself slap up against the Wall. The wall that divided the road (Route M, to the Memory Theme Park and the Mediterranean Dome) from the Wild.

The sight of it brought his heart thumping spit into his mouth. Most of Route M was lined with advertisement hoardings. The only places the Wall could be seen from the road were a few hundred yards either side of the control towers where it was made of concrete blocks topped with iron spikes. Here it was no more than a flimsy-looking wire fence that was sagging and bulging alarmingly. Electrified, almost certainly; even so, not much protection against the wilderness, the dark trees that passed thickly against it.

Tom was afraid to look. Danger stalked in those woods. Wild men lived there, barbarians and bandits, outlaws and outcasts; great hunting dogs with slavering jaws; trolls from the mountains; dragons with hot, glaring eyes. Tom's own eyes burned as he remembered the awful tales he'd been told.

Gandy spoke, in a muttering undertone. "This is the place. Must be. Nowhere else." And then, grunting, as if making an effort, "Now or never."

Tom could only hear him, not see him. The gloomy gap between the lavatory building and the fence was full of nettles that gave off a stifling smell, bitter and musty. They were tall as Tom's waist. They tangled round his knees and stung his bare hands as he pushed his way through them. Gandy's voice rose up from the ground at his feet. "Go away, Tom. *Away*. Keep away . . ."

He was lying on his back in a trench that went under the wire. His legs were on the far side of the fence that hung loose above, but not touching, his body. From the trench, his upside-down face stared up at Tom. He was covered in reddish dirt and nettle leaves. He groaned as his eyes met Tom's and said, it seemed desperately, "Clear off, there's a good lad. There's no time . . ."

And he wriggled, arms by his side, fingers digging in the earth, propelling him under the fence.

Off the road.

Tom said, "Gandy. *Grandad*. Come back."

But Gandy was up, on his feet on the other side of the fence, brushing the twigs and dirt from his trousers, shaking his head at Tom, white-faced but smiling. He sighed, shakily, turning away with a sad, shy look, a tentative, helpless wave as if saying *I'm sorry*.

Suddenly, William was shouting. "Come here, Tom. Now. This minute." And with what sounded like a sudden, choking sob, "Let Gandy *go*."

There was no time. Tom saw that clearly. No time to turn back, explain, argue with William and Penny. He had to get Gandy back before something terrible happened to him. Gandy had to be rescued because he didn't know what he was doing. He had simply gone, all of a sudden, quite bonkers. Tom understood this was something that sometimes happened when people got old. At school, in last Friday's lecture on Human Biology, his class had been told that minds wore out, just like bodies. By sixty-five most Oldies were brain-dead. Which meant, of course, that in a humane society . . .

Tom hadn't listened after that. He had put his hands over his ears. He hated the lecturer whose fat face, blown up on the big screen, was pitted with pores, like black holes. And more than her ugly mug, he hated the horrible things she told them each Friday. He didn't want to believe that all the things he did, or had done, or wanted to do, were nothing to do with *him*, nothing to do with the person he was *inside*, but were just the same things that everyone did, or wanted to do, because they were all made the same way. Human beings, rolling off the assembly line, identical living and breathing machines.

But last Friday had been the worst Friday of all because of Gandy. It had been his birthday on Saturday. And the letter had come. The letter that had made Penny cry.

Tom said hoarsely, "Hold on, Gandy, I'm coming."

He was in the trench, on his back, earth spurting under his fingers, slithering under the wire. Easier for him than for Gandy because he was so much smaller and thinner, but he was scared, all the same; if he touched the fence, even the merest touch, the electric current would go sizzling right through him. He wondered who could have dug the trench. Gandy hadn't had time. And surely the Wall was inspected regularly? Almost every day there were pictures on television showing the Trusties checking the defenses: the stout walls round the Urbs and around the roads. Keeping them all safe. Holding back the Wild.

Gandy had been a Trusty until he stopped working. Tom could just remember him in a green cap and a badge. He must have lost his wits suddenly, or he would have known what he was doing was dangerous.

By the time Tom was on his feet in the Wild

Wood, William was knee-deep in the nettles on the other side, the safe side, of the fence, his shocked face close as he dared to the wire. "Tom," he said. "*Tom*. Come back, you don't understand . . ."

Tom said, "I've got to get Gandy."

The ground between the trees was covered with spiky undergrowth, sticky brambles that tore at his clothes. He ran, stumbling and terrified. He had never been so close to wild trees before. The specimens in the Nature Parks were tamed—*denatured* was the word the Guardians used—so that their cruel, crooked branches could not reach out and catch you. All the same, it was wise not to go near them at dusk when the sap stirred inside them and they grew hungry. And at night, of course, the Nature Park gates were locked until morning. To keep people out. To keep the trees in.

Now, all around Tom, huge forest trees were rustling and murmuring, their great bushy tops swaying. It seemed to him they were talking.

Who is this boy? Trespassing in our Wild Wood. Breaking and entering. What shall we do with him? Tear him to bits? Make him one of us? Turn his legs into roots, his arms into branches . . .

A twig whipped his face and he wailed, "Gandy. Oh, please . . ."

A hand came over his mouth, an arm round his body. "Shut up," Gandy hissed in his ear.

They toppled backward together on a soft bed of leaves. Gandy whispered, "Keep still, not a sound."

The wood was full of creepings and cracklings. Tom was frozen with fright. It was true what they told you: trees were alive and malevolent. But he couldn't move, let alone run away. Gandy was holding him so tightly it was painful.

People were shouting. Men's angry voices. Someone—a woman—screamed. Then a rattle of firing.

Tom tried to struggle free but Gandy's arms were iron bars, holding him. He felt Gandy sigh. A long sigh, beneath him. Then he said, soft as another sigh, "Wait, Tom. Not too much longer."

But it seemed like hours to Tom before Gandy released him. He didn't dare speak, but he rubbed his jaw and looked at his grandfather reproachfully. Gandy paid no attention. He stood up, holding his hand out to Tom. He said, "You shouldn't have followed me off the road. You know that, don't you?"

Tom felt his mouth dry. "What'll happen? To William and Penny?"

"If you and I haven't been seen, nothing much. All that has happened is that a door was opened that should have been locked. It will have been picked up by the cameras. Now they've checked, found your father. As long as they don't know he's lost two of his passengers, they'll just tick him off for doing something he shouldn't, leave it at that. Won't investigate further."

"But someone was shooting."

"To scare, not to hurt. They don't like people snooping about near the Wall."

"I know *that*," Tom said impatiently. "They tell us at school. You might be electrocuted. Or the trees or the wild men will get you."

"Ah!" Gandy said. "Is that what they teach you? It's a long time since I was at school. But I wouldn't worry about the trees, not if I were you."

He gave Tom an odd look: part frown, part a queer little half-smile, as if there was something he wasn't sure whether to say or keep hidden. But all he said was, "The Trusties will send William and Penny packing, but they won't bother to hang about to make sure they do what they're told. Leave it half an hour or so, and you'll be able to slip back without being noticed."

"But the door will be locked again, won't it?"

"How d'you think I opened it?" Gandy said. "I hung on to a few things when I left the Service. Keys among them. Don't worry, I won't leave you until I'm sure you're back safe through the door."

Tom didn't like the sound of that. He said, "You're not *leaving* me. You're coming *with* me."

Gandy shook his head.

"But we're going to the Memory Theme Park. To take you back to your childhood. William *said!* It's your birthday treat!"

"Let's just say I changed my mind," Gandy said. "Say I heard the Call of the Wild. That I fancied a bit of an adventure at this end of my life. You forget about me, go back, go to school, take care of your parents. They've only got you."

Gandy was getting weirder and weirder, Tom thought. No two people ever had more than one child between them. It was against the law to have more. He knew, because the Friday lecturer had told him, that back in the olden days couples had sometimes produced four or five children, an unhygienic habit, or course, but they hadn't known any better. The very idea was disgusting nowadays, just as the old words *brother* and *sister* were disgusting: among the nastiest, most insulting names you could call anyone. If Gandy could say "they've only got you" as if other people might have more than one boy, or one girl, he must really be sick in his mind.

Which meant he must be looked after. Not allowed to go wandering off.

Tom said, "I won't go without you."

"You'll do as you're told," Gandy said.

He had gone red in the face as Oldies did when

you teased them, chasing after them in the street, playing the Oldies game. Tom hadn't played this game since he was six years old, which was the same year Gandy ceased to be a Trusty and became an Oldie officially. Penny had caught Tom, with some of the kids from his class, shouting after an Oldie on the street. *Wreck a Wrinkly, Pinch a Pouchy, Trip a Totterer.* She had told him to stop and although he hadn't understood at the time what he'd done wrong, he understood now. All the same, seeing the scarlet cherry spots bursting on Gandy's cheeks, and the way his mouth pursed into wrinkles, took him back to the time when he was a little boy and they'd all had such fun chasing Oldies, tormenting them until they trembled and ran away, some of them turning to shake their fists when they thought they were safe, others shaky on their skinny old legs, hunch-shouldered and weeping.

He said, six years old again suddenly, "Barmy old Bat!"

Gandy stared at him. The color went from his face. So did the anger. He took something from his pocket and tossed it on the ground between them. A key on a worn piece of leather. He said, "You'll need this. Keep it safe. The trees won't hurt you, nor the fence. It's fear they rely on."

Then he was gone, pushing his way through the

trees, trampling the undergrowth. Tom stood, stiff and still, listening until there was nothing to be heard but the small sounds of the forest: hushed sounds, snaps and swishes and flutters and sighs. Nervously, he put out a hand to touch a tree. Nothing happened; the tree didn't grab at him. But he couldn't believe it was friendly.

He wanted to go home very badly. If only he hadn't been so rude to Gandy. It wasn't Gandy's fault that he had suddenly grown old and mad. He needed to be taken care of, not insulted by his horrible grandson. If Tom couldn't look after him, at least he could say he was sorry.

As he stooped to pick up the key, he said, under his breath so nothing hostile could hear him, no tree, no wild creature, "Wait for me, Gandy, I'm coming."

Chapter 2

"Run, Gandy, run . . . *back to the forest."*

In the end, Tom had to admit he was lost. Gandy had set off at a fair lick, leaving a trail of snapped and crushed branches and grasses which made him easy to follow to start with. Tom had kept after him steadily, treading as quietly as possible, not wanting Gandy to know that he was behind him—or not before he had worked out in his mind what he was going to say when he finally reached him. Then a sudden wind had risen, whirling up flurries of last autumn's leaves like dust devils and blowing them everywhere. Tom came to a stop in a little clearing where a huge old tree had fallen. Its wood was rotten and soft, but new green shoots were growing out of its side. He picked at the rotten wood, sniffed the sweet, musty smell on his fingers, and looked round him.

There were several ways out of the clearing, but now that they were all carpeted with last autumn's leaves, there was no sign that any one of them was more likely to be the right path than another. For all Tom could tell, no one had come this way for ages. Not for years. Not for *centuries*. And there was no sign of the wind dying down. It was strong enough to make the trees groan and toss. Listening to them, Tom started to shiver.

Gandy had said there was nothing to fear from the trees. But Gandy had suddenly and mysteriously become old and mad. It was a *fact,* everyone knew it, that all trees were dangerous, even the tame trees in the Nature Parks. And here he was, lost in a huge forest of enormous wild trees, all stirring and creaking around him.

Tom started to run, not so much from the trees as from his own terror. As he ran, branches snatched at him, roots tried to trip him. Or he thought they did. But when he lost his balance, catching his foot in a bundle of roots snaking out of the ground, it was because something that was very obviously alive had started up from just under his feet with a rusty *whirr* and a flapping sound and frightened him silly.

It was only a biggish bird. A pheasant, he thought, as he fell, seeing the colored feathers out of the corner of his eye. He had seen pictures of pheasants, along with the pictures of other birds and animals, in the carnivora section of the Friday market, but he had never tasted them because his family, like the families of most of his school friends, were vegetarian. "The poor creatures lead terrible lives," his mother had told him, when he said how pretty the pheasants were. "Shut up in boxes from the minute they come out of the egg until the moment they die."

It occurred to Tom that he was beginning to be hungry. He wondered what the time was, but when he looked at his wrist he saw that his watch had gone. He looked where he'd fallen. The leaves lay light and crisp on top, old and spongy below. His fingers sank into them, stirring up a sour smell, and came out blackened with soft, oozy mud. He dug in again, wrinkling his nose at the stink, and touched the round metal case. He thought, *bit of luck, that, my being hungry, otherwise I might not have noticed I'd lost it*. Then he felt something else: a packet, or a purse, hard but not solid, more or less square.

His watch strap had broken. He shoved the grubby watch in his pocket and drew this other find out of the leaves and the mud. It was a canvas pouch, the kind that clips on to a belt. The last time Tom had seen this particular pouch, it had been bouncing on Gandy's hip as he limped (his left knee playing him up a bit) across the tarmac at the Supply Station to the Men's.

Another bit of luck, Tom thought: luck that had kept him on Gandy's track after all. Gandy could have tumbled over the roots of this same wicked old tree. The clips that fastened his pouch to his belt must have snapped, or been pulled off by brambles. At least, when he finally caught up with Gandy, he would have something to give him. It might even save him from the embarrassing business of having to say he was sorry.

Barmy old bat! Why had he said it? As grown-ups went, Gandy had sharper wits than most. Except that he was old.

The wind had dropped a little but it was beginning to rain, blowing in the wind to begin with, and then falling in earnest, heavy and straight. As long as he stayed still, he was protected by the thick forest canopy; once he started to push his way through the tangly undergrowth, water cascaded off leaves and branches, down his neck, soaking him. In the end, he crouched close to a big, sturdy tree, so glad to find he could keep almost dry under its leafy head that he forgot to be scared of it. He sat with his back against its rough but somehow comfortable and welcoming trunk, and wondered if Gandy had anything to eat in his canvas pouch.

There were two pockets, a small inner pocket and a big outer one. The bigger pocket had a folding knife, Gandy's identity card with a photograph and his DNA code, a soft, worn velvet case that had a silver compass inside, a pen, a diary, a notebook. No money. That was odd. Even odder, there was a packet of sewing needles. No thread. Just the needles. And he had never seen Gandy with a needle and thread, anyway.

Tom unzipped the inner pocket. A wallet. No money there either. Only two pictures: one of Tom's grandmother who was dead now, the other of Penny and William, standing outside the back door at home, Tom between them. Looking at their friendly faces smiling up at him, Tom whistled under his breath to stop himself crying. He wished he had said good-bye.

There was something else in the pocket. A piece of paper folded small. He unfolded it, and words in black capital letters leaped out at him.

JAMES MAKEPEACE JACOBS.

That was Gandy's name. This must be the letter. The one he had not been allowed to see. Gandy's letter, that had dropped on the mat on Saturday morning.

He had gone to pick it up, thinking it might be

a birthday card for Gandy from one of his funny old friends. But Penny had heard the *thump* of the post and come running. She had pushed Tom aside, picked up the letter, and without looking at him, without speaking, gone into the kitchen and closed the door in his face. She had never done anything like that before. He wondered what was wrong, if it was somehow his fault. Then he had heard her crying. He thought he might go and say he was sorry, just in case he had done something to hurt her, but when he opened the door of the kitchen she had smiled at him, just a little bit shakily, and said, "All right now, darling, it was just Gandy's letter, I knew it was coming but it was a shock, all the same."

That was all she would say. She had put the letter in her pocket which was odd, he thought, since she had said *Gandy's letter,* but he understood now.

The letter was meant for his parents. For his mother, whose name was Penelope, and for his father, whose name was William. But it was about Gandy.

Dear William and Penelope:
   On June 12, 2040 JAMES MAKEPEACE JACOBS will be 65, his last day of work having been completed on December 21, 2035.

Your work as carers for your father/father-in-law/friend has been admirable, and has been properly recognized in generous tax allowances and grants. The time has come for him to move on and your final task is now to enroll him in Nostalgia Block 95 of your nearest Memory Theme Park. You and your son/daughter will accompany him to the Park and you will spend two days and one night all together enjoying the total reality of the 1980s and 1990s. When you leave him he will be gently and permanently cared for under Stat.1066/01/0S5.

Thank you for your good work. You are expected at the Park Induction Office at 16.30.

Tom read this letter twice. Then a third time. When he had finished he folded it up again, put it very slowly and carefully back in the pouch, and put the pouch in the inside pocket of his jacket.

He decided not to think about what it meant for the moment. There was something menacing about it, a blackness lurking at the edge of his mind that he preferred not to look at. The letter had made Penny cry. Was that why Gandy had brought it with him? Tucked it away in his pouch so she would forget all about it?

He told himself that whatever the letter meant, Gandy would explain it once he had found him. Gandy was always good at explaining. Better than Penny and William. Of course, being an Oldie, he had more time to spare. All Oldies stopped work on their sixtieth birthday and although they were usually charged with the care of the family child while its parents were working, most people considered they had an easy life. Free beer, a free trip once a year to a Dome or a Theme Park. And then, at sixty-five, as the letter had said, cared for "permanently."

Tom thought, *of course! That's* what the letter meant! The Memory Theme Parks were where Oldies went when they needed to be looked after forever, not just a Sunday treat for a sixty-fifth birthday. Was that why Penny had cried? Because Gandy was leaving them? But she must have known. She had been expecting the letter.

The rain had stopped. The trees were still dripping but shafts of sunlight stretched down through their branches, making the spaces between them seem more open and friendly. Tom got up slowly, still wondering about his mother and Gandy's letter, but with enough of his mind roaming free to realize that ahead of him the trees were, in fact, thinning out; in the distance, a bright wall of sunshine marked the end of the forest.

Tom felt his heart lift. He wasn't as scared of the trees as he had been to begin with, but he would be glad to be out of them all the same. Afternoon would turn into evening and it wasn't only trees that would come to life then but all the other creatures that lived in the forest: real, savage animals like wolves and wild boars, as well as the trolls and the dragons that he no longer *really* believed in while the sun was still brightly shining, but might change his mind about once it grew dark.

He set off at a good pace. It was much easier walking now, and he was feeling more cheerful. He had no real reason to suppose that he would find Gandy soon—if not in the next five minutes, at least within the next hour—but he was comfortably sure it would not be long, all the same. Gandy liked the sun. Once he was out of the wood, Tom would probably find him sitting on a fallen tree, or lying flat on his back on the grass, his eyes closed and his beard pointing to the sky. (Gandy was fairly short of hair on his head but his black beard and his bushy eyebrows were stiff and luxuriant.)

Instead, he was on his feet, talking . . .

Tom saw the others first, and froze still. The Wild Men—the outlaws, the barbarians—were the biggest danger of all. They roamed the wilderness looking for foolish children who had slipped off the road, away from their parents, thinking it might be an adventure to see what lay on the other side of the Wall. They were cannibals. They were ten feet tall. Their naked bodies were covered in hair. They had an extra long, sharp tooth on each side of their slobby, glistening mouths and their hands ended in black, vicious claws.

But the three barbarians standing round Gandy were nothing like that. They were about Gandy's height. Their hair was long, falling to their shoulders, but as far as Tom could tell, it was confined to their heads. Their bodies were hidden under curious, rather rough-looking clothes made of a thick, grayish-green material: baggy trousers and a loose, belted jacket or shirt.

Tom crouched behind a bush and strained to hear what Gandy was saying.

Gandy was patting his hip, showing them something. Something broken, where the pouch had been fastened? Then he turned, waved a hand, pointing back at the forest. Laughing. Shrugging his shoulders.

One of the barbarians was talking now. Gandy was leaning forward, listening intently. He put his hand to his ear to show that he was a bit deaf and the barbarian raised his voice so that Tom was able to hear him.

He said, "Unfortunately, without proof . . . You must understand. We will have to arrest you."

He took Gandy's arm in a way that looked rough to Tom. He shot to his feet and charged. He thudded head first into the barbarian's belly, hitting him so hard that he gasped and let Gandy go. Tom flung his arms round the barbarian's waist and shouted, "Run, Gandy, *run* . . . get back to the forest . . ."

Chapter 3

"The last map of the real world . . ."

The barbarian was laughing. Pressed against his belly, Tom could feel it wobbling with laughter. Then his elbows were seized, strong thumbs dug painfully into his muscles, and he was thrust away, to be held at arm's length with a brown, bristly face grinning down at him.

The barbarian said, "Who's the boy, James Makepeace Jacobs? Seems to belong to you, doesn't he? Another illegal?"

He let Tom go. But he stood between Tom and the forest. And the other two barbarians, stationed either side of Gandy, close but not touching, were clearly on guard.

Gandy said, speaking slowly, his eyes holding Tom's, "Until an hour ago, I'd not set eyes on this lad in my life. But I can tell you who he is. Thomas Jacobs, my brother's boy. Come to meet his old uncle, all the way from Owlbury Hall Farm. That's Montgomery way. The Welsh Marches. Not far from Offa's Dyke, I seem to remember."

Tom stared at him. Gandy stared back, his gaze hard and unblinking, and Tom knew he had to keep quiet and say nothing. At least until he understood what was happening.

Gandy said, with a laugh that showed his long, yellow teeth, "May be the first time I'd seen him, but I knew him at once. No doubt about it! Spitting image of my young brother!"

The laughing barbarian, who was not laughing now, looked at Tom thoughtfully. He didn't seem shocked or insulted by the coarse way Gandy kept using the disgusting word *brother* but Tom was sure he knew Gandy was lying.

Gandy said, "You know, I wondered where you'd got to, Thomas. If I hadn't come across the Ranger here, I'd have turned back to look for you."

Tom answered in as innocent a voice as he could manage, "You dropped your pouch, Uncle. That's what I went back for. I saw it come off your belt. You didn't notice."

He took the pouch out of his pocket and handed it over. He saw Gandy's fingers were trembling as he unfastened it, and hoped the barbarians didn't notice. He looked cautiously at them. Although their clothes were rough-looking and they had a strange, earthy smell about them, as if they had not been through the deodorizer this morning, they didn't look particularly wild or dangerous. Just like ordinary men, in fact. No fangs. No talons. Two of them were young, with smooth, rosy cheeks; the third, the one who had laughed, the only one who had spoken so far, was much older, Tom thought. Older, even, than Gandy.

"Here it is," Gandy said. He was holding the letter. The older barbarian took it and read it, holding it at arm's length, as if there were a bad smell about it.

Gandy said, after a minute, "All the evidence you need, I think?"

The man took a pen from his pocket and scribbled on the bottom of the letter. He said, "That should do for now. See the Rangers' Office in Montgomery when you get there. You'll need to have it confirmed officially, all the right stamps, that sort of bureaucratic fuss, but I shouldn't think there's any doubt you're entitled to asylum."

He gave Gandy the letter and said, "There but for the grace of God . . ." He stopped, and sighed. Then laughed, as he had laughed earlier. With a bit of an edge to his laughter. He reached out to touch the collar of Tom's Wonderclean shirt, rubbing the material between his thumb and forefinger. He said, "Keep an eye on your nephew, Mr. Jacobs. Other Rangers may not be as indulgent."

The way the barbarian—the *Ranger*—looked at Gandy, sharp and sly, made Tom tremble. This was someone who was quick to change: nice one minute, nasty the next. The sooner he and Gandy were out of his reach the better.

He guessed Gandy thought so too. But Gandy took his time about replacing the folded letter in the pouch and fastening the pouch to his belt. Then he narrowed his eyes and said—as casually as if he were asking the way in a strange Urb—"How long d'you think it'll take us? The boy here did it in the day but he's got young legs."

Tom thought, *a day's march!* Chasing after Gandy today, he'd walked further than he had ever done in his life. The longest he ever walked normally was four or five minutes to the end of the road to catch the School Pedalator. These moving pavements sometimes broke down, but when that happened you simply waited in one of the shelters until the Engineers came to repair them. No one *walked*—unless you counted climbing in the Mountaineering Theme Park going for a walk. Sometimes people strolled in the Nature Park but most preferred to view the exhibits from the comfort and safety of the circular railway, the tilting Pendolino train.

The Ranger said, "With a bit of luck you'll pick up a carrier. Bishop's Castle has a market on Mondays so there's plenty of readying up at the weekend, folk coming and going. And since your young nephew here knows the country, you shouldn't have any difficulty."

He was looking at Tom as he spoke, rubbing his chin with his forefinger. Tom said, quickly, his heart thumping about in his chest like a heavy ball, "If you get tired, Uncle James, we can stop and rest. Or, like the Ranger says, we might meet a—a carrier."

He wondered what a "carrier" was. Something that carried you, obviously. But what kind of something? An electric cart? A hydrogen car?

Gandy said, "We'd best be getting on then, young Tom."

He put one hand on Tom's shoulder and lifted the other in solemn farewell. Tom felt his grandfather's fingers digging into his shoulder, turning him, guiding him. He held his breath as they walked away from the Rangers. He thought he could feel their eyes boring into his back. Any moment there would be shouting, heavy feet pounding after them . . .

Nothing happened. Gandy led him out of the

clearing, through a belt of young trees to a narrow dirt road, a track of rutted earth. Gandy said, softly, "Don't look back. Just keep going, there's a good lad, and pray this is the right direction you're taking me. We don't want to make that Ranger any more suspicious than he is already. With a bit of luck we should be out of his sight in a minute. Though not out of his mind, I fear."

Tom whispered, "They're just ordinary people."

Gandy laughed shortly. "Not ogres with one green eye in the middle of their forehead? I suppose boys your age really do believe that old nonsense."

He sounded contemptuous. Tom said, angry suddenly, "Why did you tell all those lies? About me being your . . ." He couldn't bring himself to say the rude word Gandy had used. Instead he said, lamely, "I mean, *not* being your grandson."

Gandy said, "I reckoned they'd let me pass. As the Ranger said, we Oldies are bound to be given asylum. But we are a special case. I have the feeling they may not be so keen on taking in younger folk *off the road*. What they'd call *from Inside*. Upsets the balance here. On the Outside."

"Is that what *they* call it *here*? What we call the Wild?"

Gandy nodded. "Different names, different ways of looking at things. You can say *brother* this side of the Wall, in the Wild, without shocking

37

anyone! On the Outside it's normal to have brothers and sisters. Even for people your age."

"*What?* Why—" Tom began but Gandy waved a hand, hushing him.

"Bit at a time," he said. "There's too much to take in all at once. Besides, I'm not sure I can tell you all you might want to know. I've been Inside too long myself. We'll have to find out a lot of answers together."

Tom said, "Just one question, then. Where are we going?" He was feeling so queer suddenly, shaky-legged and sick. His tongue was numb and his lips were buzzing. It was as if he couldn't wake up from a nightmare. Or *had* woken up and found he was still trapped inside it.

Gandy stopped. The track they were following was climbing steadily. They had left the trees behind and were on high ground, on a bare, open mountain; the sun shone down on thin, starved-looking grass and great, gray, rocky outcrops. Some of the bigger rocks on the mountain summit had dark openings in them. *Caves,* Tom thought. The sort of caves where trolls might live. Or ogres. He started to shiver.

Gandy said, "Look here. I'll try and show you."

He had taken something out of his back pocket and began to unfold it slowly and carefully. At first Tom thought it was just an ordinary map of the

Urbs and the Routes but then he saw it was unlike any map he had ever seen. There were no blank white spaces on either side of the straight red roads that led from the Urbs to the Theme Parks. This map was colored all over, green and brown, and had wavy lines drawn on it and names written everywhere, some in big letters, some in small.

This strange map was old and delicate, worn and scuffed in the creases. Gandy crouched on his hunkers and carefully spread it out on the ground. "Take a look," he said. "My Grandad gave this to me before he died. I've taken good care of it. That's how I lost the pouch, I suppose. I took a tumble and was too keen to make sure I'd still got the map in my back pocket to check on anything else."

He stroked the map lovingly and said, in a reverent voice, "This must be just about the last map of the real world in existence."

Tom stared at it. He said, "Why's it all written on? And why is some green and some brown?"

"Brown is the mountains, green is the lowland. Those wavy lines are contours. They show how the land falls and rises. And the writing is the names of all the towns and the villages in this part of the country. Even most of the houses. It's an old Ordnance Survey map. Illegal, of course, since the millennium."

"Where's our Urb? Where is Urb Seven?"

Tom felt his mind spinning out of control. If this peculiar map had Urb Seven printed upon it, he could anchor himself in what Gandy called the "real world." At least have a shot at it.

Gandy said, "Urb Seven's way off this map. It was called Birmingham in the old days. We'd come some way down Route M, when we stopped. We should be about here. Not far from Ludlow."

Gandy's finger, pointing out this name on the map, was trembling. But not from fear. When Gandy looked up, Tom saw the tears in his eyes. Gandy said, "Ludlow used to be a lovely old town. Wonder what it's like now."

Tom said, "Where's Route M?"

"It wasn't built then. Oh, there were some big straight roads, motorways they were called, but nothing like the Routes. Nothing so ugly and— and, oh, nothing so *hopeless!* The motorways led somewhere worth seeing."

Gandy's tears had spilled over and were rolling slowly down his cheeks.

Tom was sorry for Gandy, sorry he was feeling so sad, but he was also scared for himself. How would he manage if he suddenly had to take care of his grandfather? Grown-ups, even Oldies, should look after children, not the other way round. He knelt beside Gandy and patted his cheeks with soft little taps. He said, "Don't cry,

Gandy. What can I do to make you feel better? Where d'you want to go? Show me on the map. Or do you want to go back? I'll do whatever you want. Only, please, don't cry. Please don't be unhappy."

Gandy rubbed his nose with the back of his hand as if it were itching. He was laughing now, laughing and sniffing. He said, "Not unhappiness, lad. Quite the reverse, in fact. Happy memories. My brother, my brother Jack and I, used to spend summers in this part of the country when I was your age. My uncle, that was my father's brother, he had a farm and we had a rare old time on it. Uncle let us roam, wild as goats. Clear off, he'd say, bit of bread and cheese in your pockets to stop you getting clemmed, and come back when you're ready. It was that farm Jack was aiming for when he left."

"Left what? Where? I don't understand."

But Gandy had slipped away from the present, slipped back in time; all he was listening to was an old story unfolding inside his head.

"Jack was six years younger than I was, a single man, free to go. I should have gone with him, but Lisa was too afraid. She liked an easy life and she was always a timid girl. Not one to risk anything. And William was only a baby."

Lisa had been Gandy's wife. She had died before

Tom was born but he had seen her photograph in Gandy's room. Tom tugged at Gandy's sleeve to bring him back to the present. He said, "You mean, Jack left our Urb long ago, to come here, into the Wild? When William was a baby, so you couldn't leave him?"

Gandy nodded. "Well, there was *my* father too. I had him to look after as well. Your great-grandad. He couldn't stand what was going on, human life turned to profit and loss, but he was a schoolmaster. Even if he couldn't put a stop to it, he thought he could at least try to tell the truth to the kids he was teaching. He couldn't do it, and it broke him. I saw it break him. The children reported him to their parents and their parents reported him to the Protectors. When he was—was *taken*—then I could have gone after Jack, made Lisa come with me, but the Wall was going up. And the ugly stories had started."

Gandy sighed. He stood up, his knees cracking. He folded the map to look at one section more closely. He said, "I think if we keep on this track, over the mountain, we should pick up the Bishop's Castle road through the valley . . ."

Tom said, "What did he want to put a stop to? Your Dad?"

Gandy looked at him thoughtfully. "First things first," he said. "And very much first, I think, is to do something about the unsuitable clothes you are wearing. That shirt shrieks *Inside*."

Tom looked down at his spotless shirt. "It doesn't get dirty."

"That was my meaning." Gandy was grinning. "That sort of miracle gear is likely to make you look conspicuous in the Outside. I don't suppose you noticed but I am wearing a remarkably ancient pair of trousers. Happened to find them in the back of my cupboard."

"I noticed," Tom said. "You meant to go off the road, didn't you? All along. Did you tell Dad and Penny?"

"They may have guessed. We didn't discuss it." Gandy jerked up his chin, thrusting his black beard sharply forward the way he did when he had made up his mind to get on with something. He said, "Now then, Tom lad, cut the cackle, we've a fair way to go before nightfall."

And he set off at a brisk pace. Tom had to run to keep up with him and found himself too short of breath to carry on talking. But that didn't stop him keeping a sharp watch around him. Gandy might believe the Wild was not dangerous but it was still important that Tom kept his eyes open. Even if Gandy was right and some of the warnings children were given about savage trees and wild men with long fangs and talons were just "ugly stories,"

Gandy was too old to be trusted. Oldies became loose in their wits, that was what they were told at school. Not everything they'd been taught was wrong, surely? And Gandy had certainly been acting strangely . . .

As he was acting now.

They had reached the top of a steep rise and were starting down into a valley. From halfway down the next slope, beyond a clump of trees, came the sound of splashing and shouting. Boys' voices, and the roar of water. Gandy said, "Ha!"— and set off at a run.

Tom followed him. When Gandy reached the trees, he stopped and crouched low. He flapped his hand behind him to tell Tom to get down, and crept forward slowly. Beyond the trees, a waterfall tumbled into a rocky hollow, making a natural swimming pool. Young, naked barbarians—Tom counted seven but there might have been more— were leaping in and out of the water, diving off the rocks, jumping in and out of the hissing curtain of spray, shrieking and splashing each other.

Gandy whispered in Tom's ear, "What a bit of luck! Take off the fancy shirt, will you . . ."

Tom stared, bewildered.

Gandy was on his belly now, wriggling toward the piles of clothes abandoned in the trees. He picked up one garment, then another. Taking his time, Tom thought, sick with fear. Gandy was only partly hidden by the trees. Any minute one of the barbarians might turn and see him . . .

But he was back before Tom was out of his Wonderclean shirt. Gandy tugged at his collar, wrenching it off him. "Get a move on," he hissed. "We need to get out of here."

He thrust Tom's arms into the arms of the rough gray shirt he was holding. The shirt he had *stolen,* Tom thought, with dread.

Chapter 4

Mr. Simon Watkins, Carrier, Newsbearer . . .

Gandy said, "We'd better get out of here pronto."

And he was off at once, strong, skinny legs moving like pistons. Trying to keep up with him, Tom's muscles ached and his chest felt as if it might burst. But fear of the naked barbarian boys drove him on. He could still hear them distantly splashing and screaming, safely out of sight by now, but all that leaping about, in and out of cold water, must be terribly tiring. Any minute one of them might decide he'd had enough, get out of the water, find his shirt gone . . .

There were no thieves in the Urbs since the outlaws and the barbarians had been driven away. No one needed to steal. Everyone had all they wanted or needed, which was exactly the same things as everyone else. To take from another person would be a terrible act of ingratitude against the Protectors who kept them all housed and fed—and safe from the Wild.

Tom said breathlessly, stumbling into Gandy who had stopped suddenly, "It's wrong to steal."

"Exchange is no robbery," Gandy said. "And that boy's mother will reckon she's got a good bargain. But we don't want the fancy shirt traced to you, all the same. Just you remember you're Thomas Jacobs from Owlbury Hall, and you've worn good homespun clothes all your life."

Tom wriggled inside the barbarian's shirt. "It's prickly," he said. "Itchy."

"Well, you'll have to put up with it," Gandy said bracingly. "And learn to shift a bit faster or we won't get where we want to go before nightfall."

"My legs *hurt*," Tom grumbled. "You just go too fast for me. It's not fair, you've had *practice*."

He remembered how odd he had thought it when Gandy did what he called "working out" in the yard at the back of the house. Tom had always been nervous in case one of his friends should turn up and catch Gandy at it, touching his toes, doing press-ups, waving his arms about. Only kids, little kids, too young to understand taking exercise was a waste of time, ran about, playing.

Gandy grinned. "I'm sorry, I'm sure! Oh, it's not your fault you're so feeble. I'm not blaming you. I should have got stuck into training you up a bit earlier. But Penny might have noticed. And wondered."

Tom felt as if he had been picked up by a giant hand and dropped from a great height. He drew a huge, shuddery breath. He stuttered. "*G-Gandy!*"

He saw it all now. Gandy had been a Trusty. He had been trained to lock doors behind him. The door in the Men's had been marked NO EXIT. Gandy would never have left it open unless he had meant to. So he must have guessed Tom was likely to follow him.

Tom said, "You meant me to come with you all along. Didn't you?"

Gandy was rubbing his nose. It was something he often did when he was thinking. He said, "Perhaps. I may have had it in mind. I was half for it, half not. Reasons for and against. I don't know."

He looked at Tom and sighed. "I suppose I thought you ought to see what went on Outside. In the real world—a different world, anyway. But it's a dangerous business, finding things out. And besides, were you up to it? I had to ask myself that."

Tom said, indignantly, "Why didn't you tell me? You might have just *asked*. I might have just liked to make up my own mind! And what d'you mean, was I *up to it?*"

He expected his grandfather to apologize. Oldies were not supposed to criticize children! And Gandy had been more than critical. He had been plain insulting!

But Gandy was chuckling. "Don't take offense now. It isn't your *character* I was doubting. Just, could you *keep up* with me? All that sitting about! Are your *legs* up to it? Life's more physical, you'll find, this side of the Wall. Off the road."

"I keep my energy for thinking," Tom said, repeating what his teachers had told him. "Your mind uses up calories just as much as your body, and if you run about all the time you don't have much power left for brainstorming."

Although Gandy nodded gravely, as if he took this point seriously, Tom looked at his mouth and saw a smile struggling hard to get out. He said, hastily, "I can keep up all right. Long as you don't go too fast. And it's not too far. How far is it? Where we're going. This place, it won't really take all day, will it? To get there?"

But Gandy wasn't paying attention. He had cupped one hand behind an ear. "Quiet," he said. "Quiet, lad. Listen."

At first, Tom could only hear the cries of the barbarian children and those were faint now, no more than a cottony whisper, like thistles blowing on the wind. Then he heard a new sound, a squeaking and creaking, a bit of a rumble. Iron. Something like that. Some kind of metal.

The rumble grew louder. And the squeaking and creaking and cracking, and then a deep panting sound: the sound of a very large animal heavily breathing. And coming closer.

Trolls, Tom thought, a hideous troll coming to get us, huge feet shod with iron, savage eyes shooting fire and great glistening mouth hanging open . . .

A whimper escaped him. He closed his eyes and stood close to Gandy.

"It's all right, Tomkin," Gandy said, very gentle-voiced suddenly. "It's only the carrier cart. With a bit of luck you'll be able to save your poor old legs for another day."

Tom opened his eyes. For a nanosecond what he saw was as terrifying to him as any troll would have been: an immense, long head, tossing up and down, snorting smoke from its nostrils, wild, white eyes rolling. But then, almost at once (or, to be exact, in a thousand-millionth of a second), his mind sorted out what he saw and turned it into a horse: a big, brown horse, steaming and sweating, four massive feet shifting and stamping.

Only a horse. All the same, he was glad Gandy

had an arm round him. Tom had seen quiet, tame horses, giving children rides in the Pleasure Dome, but he had never been so close to one before. And although this horse was wearing leather harness and so couldn't be really wild, it didn't look all that tame, either. It stretched its gleaming neck toward Tom, soft lips nuzzling so close to Tom's hand that he felt its hot breath. He shrank back, against Gandy.

"Arter a bit of apple, that's all, boy," a voice said. A very deep, laughing voice with a bit of a rasp to it that sounded as if it must belong to an enormous man with a great barrel chest. But the only person it could have come from, as far as Tom could see, was a tiny, shrunken, goblin-like person, perched on the driver's seat at the front of the cart with his little boots propped on the rail in front of him and his little hands holding the horse's reins on his knees. He had long, loose white hair and a soft, bulky white beard that hid most of his face and from which his dark eyes peeked out, bright as a bird's in a thicket.

He said, his deep voice rolling like thunder, "Simon Watkins, Carrier, Postman, and News-bearer. At your service."

Tom gaped at him. This was the most ancient man he had ever seen in his life. Very few of the Oldies had white hair in the Urbs; most of them took a pill to keep the color in. And he had never seen anyone with such thin, bony fingers. It was as if only the fat blue veins, snaking over the backs of his hands, held them fastened together.

Gandy said, "James Makepeace Jacobs. And my brother's boy, Thomas Jacobs from Owlbury Hall. Any chance you might lift us a piece of the way?"

Simon Watkins's eyes held a sparkly amusement that made Tom uneasy. He said, "I deliver to Owlbury. I didn't know as Jack Jacobs had such a young lad. All his boys are full-grown and hearty, I thought. Though I'm getting on, mind, cogs a bit rusty, you expect that, my age. How old d'you think I am, Thomas Jacobs?"

Tom shook his head. Oldies didn't ask children questions like that in the Urbs. He didn't know how he should answer.

Simon Watkins laughed—a laugh to match his giant's voice. It made the mountains ring. He said, "It's all right, laddie. It may seem a bit odd where you've come from, but we're proud to be old around here. You won't insult me by saying I'm ninety, any more than you'd flatter me saying I'm still a young man in my fifties!"

Tom's heart sank. Simon Watkins knew he was a stranger. That he'd come from the Inside. An Illegal—wasn't that what the Ranger had said? And if this funny old man had realized Tom was an Illegal

Insider before he had even opened his mouth, what chance had he got of getting by on the Outside? He was bound to be caught and sent back—or worse! What "worse" might mean on the Outside, he preferred not to think about.

It was no use relying on Gandy to cover up for him. Gandy had already made a stupid mistake, saying Tom was his brother's boy, forgetting that his brother Jack would be almost as old as he was by now, with grandchildren Tom's age.

Tom looked at Gandy and saw the color rise in his face as he said, "Of course, Jack was younger than me. By a good many years."

It seemed to Tom that in trying to explain, Gandy had made it worse, not better. Simon Watkins was grinning evilly, showing a mouth that had only a few teeth remaining, leaning crookedly against each other.

He said, "Don't you mind me. I'm just a carrier. Letters, vegetables, livestock, people. I don't ask questions. Discretion's my middle name. Simon Discreet Watkins, that's me. You can ride beside me, James Makepeace Jacobs, but the lad better get in the back, ready to dive under the sacks, just in case we run into someone less easy-going."

Gandy's hand was on Tom's back, giving him a little push forward.

Tom said, "Thank you, Mr. Watkins. I'm sure

we are much obliged to you, sir."

Simon Watkins laughed his giant's laugh. "Glad to hear you've a tongue in your head, young man. And someone has taught you pretty manners at least. Do you need a hand up, Mr. Jacobs?"

The floor of the high-sided wooden cart was crowded: lumpy sacks of what Tom guessed were potatoes, softer bags of what seemed to be a rough sort of flour, a crate of squawking chickens, parcels of all shapes and sizes, and nestling among them, a man's dusty old cap, full of large speckled eggs.

"Careful of them duck eggs, young man," Simon Watkins said. "Mrs. Davies, below the Bent Hill, she wants them to put under a broody hen, I promised particular."

"What d'you think I was going to do?" Tom muttered under his breath. "*Tread* on them?"

Gandy shot him a stern look over his shoulder and then said, loudly, "I used to know a family Davies, lived over Welshpool way. There was a boy called Emlyn, much my age, and a girl, Harriet, I think, a bit younger."

"You've just missed young Emlyn. Passed away a week ago." To Tom's surprise, Simon Watkins chuckled. "His father's my age and still going strong; you see these young chaps falling off their perch in their sixties, it makes us old 'uns feel immortal. Harriet Davies is the one wants the eggs.

I call her Mrs. out of respect, but she never wed. She keeps house for her father and raises poultry and grows vegetables; I daresay I'll be picking up a good load of cooking greens when I deliver the eggs."

This was boring, Tom thought, so he stopped listening. He had enough to do, anyway, trying to make himself comfortable among the lumpy sacks of potatoes and working out how he could hide if he had to. In the end, he settled himself at the far end of the cart, well away from the eggs and the chickens, tucking himself under some empty sacks and having one handy to pull over his face in an emergency. He hoped Gandy or Mr. Watkins would tell him when he had to take cover. At the moment they just seemed to be chuntering on about people Gandy had known back in the Dark Ages. Before the Urbs and the Roads were built. Before the Wall went up. Before the Millennium . . .

Actually, as Tom worked it out, they were talking about a time when Gandy had been roughly Tom's age. For a little while, Tom tried to put himself forward to a time when he would be the same age as Gandy, and talking about who he'd known and how he'd felt when he was the age he was now, eleven going on twelve, but it was too complicated and he began to feel sleepy.

Sleepy and sleepier . . .

It was easier than he would have expected to fall

asleep under a lot of smelly sacks in a rackety old cart that was lurching and grinding along, in and out of rough ruts in the road. The rumble and squeak of the big, iron-rimmed wheels was a soothing sound as he got used to it. Rumble, rumble, squeak, rumble, squeak, rumble, rumble . . .

When he woke, squeak-rumble had stopped. Instead, what he heard was a juicy chewing and champing. The cart shifted a bit, back and forth, but it wasn't going anywhere. Tom lay still for a minute, and then sat up cautiously to peep over the side of the cart. It was parked in a deep sunken lane with high hedges and trees to either side and the big brown horse was tearing at the grass on the bank. The lane curved in front and behind; all Tom could see were hedges and sky. There was no sign of Gandy and Simon Watkins.

He stood up in the cart and the big brown horse turned its head to look at him. It had a mild and inquiring expression and Tom felt foolish as he remembered how scared he had been of it earlier. He said, "It's all right, you just go on eating, I don't want you to take me anywhere."

His voice sounded terribly loud to him and that made him feel even sillier. At least there was no one around to hear him talking to this gentle beast as if it were human . . .

But he was wrong about that. Someone said,

"You're awake, then. Great-Uncle James said to let you sleep so I've been getting bored up in this tree."

He looked up and saw her, a girl about his own age with long black hair and a small, fierce face. Like an owl, Tom thought, remembering a baby owl he had seen in Urb Seven's Natural History Dome, with its little hooked nose and clear, polished eyes. She was lying along the branch of a tree, legs dangling either side. She looked perfectly calm and comfortable as if she had no idea of the danger she was in.

He said, "Please come down. Trees can be vicious."

She looked at him blankly and Tom was afraid for her.

He said, "You never know what they are going to do. I mean, that tree is quiet now but it might make up its mind to throw you off any minute."

No reaction except an even more astonished stare. Then she swung herself off the branch, dropped lightly to a lower one, and then to the ground. She shook her fist at the tree and said, "You watch it, old tree, or I'll get my Dad to cut you down before you kill again!" She turned to Tom and giggled. "Great-Uncle James said I'd find you had some peculiar notions. You potty, or what?"

Tom shook his head. He had just been through

a whole wood of trees without being attacked. And now he thought about it, no one he knew had ever been harmed by a tree. He said, "I'm sorry, it's just an old tale someone told me. How do I know if it's true or not?"

This girl looked quite *nice,* he thought, sympathetic. As if she might understand, if he could ever explain to her. He said, "How do you know when things grown-ups tell you are true?"

She said nothing, only frowned, but he could see she was thinking. Taking him seriously? Or perhaps she was just deciding he must be mad.

He said, embarrassed suddenly, "Who are you? What's your name?"

"Liz," she said. "Lizzie, if you prefer. Or Elizabeth. After a Queen there was once. Your grandfather is my Great-Uncle James. I'm your second cousin."

"What's a cousin?" Tom asked and was even more embarrassed when she started to laugh.

Chapter 5

"Never after dark . . ."

He thought she would never stop laughing. In the end, he got out of the cart and turned his back on her and marched away up the lane.

She ran after him and whirled round in front of him. She said, "Oh, I'm sorry. It was mean to laugh . . ."

She was trying so hard to keep a straight face. Her cheeks were tight and red as apples. She said, her voice quivering, "A cousin is a relation. You know what a relation is, don't you?"

Tom said stiffly, "I'm not totally ignorant. A relation is a person who belongs to your family. A mother or a father or a grandparent."

"A cousin's just a bit further away. Cousins are the children of your mother's and father's brothers and sisters, who are your uncles and aunts. And second cousins like you and me are the grandchildren of our grandparents' brothers and sisters. Like, your grandfather and my grandfather being brothers."

She spoke the dirty words *brother* and *sister* perfectly calmly. They were obviously not insults to her, but the same sort of words as *uncle* and *aunt* and *cousin*.

He said, cautiously, "You mean all these words . . ." He hesitated, wondering how to put it. He couldn't bring himself to say *brother* or *sister*. He said, "I mean, the uncle and aunt words, are the same sort of words as mother and father? I mean, you don't—you don't think they're *rude?*"

He was afraid she was going to laugh again. But she didn't. She looked, suddenly, oddly shy. She said, very gentle and patient, "They can't be rude, can they? They're just words to describe how people belong to each other. I think you better come and meet the rest of your family."

She took his hand as if she'd known him all his life. Her hand was small and warm and grubby and as they walked together along the lane, Tom caught a whiff of her sweat. It wasn't as unpleasant as he would have expected. In fact he probably smelled a bit himself by now after lying under those filthy old sacks. He took a quick sniff at his armpit and confirmed this suspicion. He thought his smell was different from Lizzie's. And the barbarian Ranger had smelled different again. He wondered if people on the Outside recognized each other by their individual smells . . .

He thought of a way to get his own back on Lizzie.

He said, "I don't suppose you know what a deodorizer is?"

She shook her head. She didn't seem to mind not knowing. He said, "It's, like, sanitation. You step through in the morning and it takes your bad smells away."

"You smell okay to me," she said cheerfully. "You think *I* stink? Is that what you're trying to tell me?"

"Of course not!" Although it was exactly what he had meant, he was ashamed to hear her say it. And astonished that she didn't seem to mind. She let go his hand, but it was only to push open a wide wooden gate. "Here we are," she said. "Owlbury Hall."

Beyond the gate was a yard, a farmyard with stables and horses looking out over the doors, and a well, and a pump, and an open-sided barn with carts resting on their shafts, and what Tom recognized as an old wooden plow. He had seen one just like it in the Virtual Reality Theme Park, in the

Olden Days Section. Several baby pigs trotted inquisitively about with cardboard collars round their necks, chickens scratched in the dirt, and a bitch got up from her place in the shade of a tree and came toward them, creeping belly-low, wagging her plumed tail and smiling.

Tom had been to the Virtual Reality Theme Park two years ago on a school visit that was part of the history course. He assumed that beyond these old farm buildings there would be other displays: an ancient stone castle, or an old city, with stinking sewers running down the middle of the narrow streets and the rancid reek of decaying fish or meat in the market. The Theme Park instructor had kept on pointing out how uncomfortable and dirty and smelly the old Urbs had been before deodorizers and refrigerators had been discovered. It had been almost as if, Tom thought suddenly, the only purpose of their visit to the Theme Park was to make sure they all realized how lucky they were to live in clean, tidy Urbs with proper sanitation and hygiene.

Tom said, "Where's your Urb, Lizzie? I mean, where you live?"

"Here of course," she said. She looked a bit puzzled, but then her face cleared. "Not in the stables, is that what you thought? No, we all live in the house."

They had turned the corner of the big open barn and the house was in front of them, a large old house with a low stone wall around it and within the stone wall, a strip of garden full of flowers. Gandy was sitting on a bench against the wall of the house, looking up at the man standing beside him, one foot on the bench, a pipe in his mouth.

"That man's *smoking*," Tom said, shocked.

"Oh, he always smokes. Grows his own baccy," Lizzie said calmly. "That's my grandfather. Your Great-Uncle Jack. You remember what I told you? How families fit together?"

"I remember," Tom said.

Gandy waved to him. "There you are, Tomkin! Lizzie taken good care of you?"

He stood up from the bench, as Tom pushed open a little green gate in the stone wall, and put his hand on Tom's shoulder. "Here he is, Jack," he said, proudly. "My grandson Thomas. Called Tom. He's a good lad. And a brave one. Came after me, to take care of me, though he was scared almost witless."

Although Jack was younger than Gandy, he had gray hair and a lined, wind-battered face. He looked like Gandy, all the same, not feature by feature, just something to do with the way his eyes screwed up at the corners, the way he was frowning. Gandy frowned like that, too. It must be strange to have a brother, Tom thought. Someone like you, and yet not alike . . .

Jack was still frowning. He took his pipe out of his mouth and stroked his nose with its stem, the way Gandy stroked his nose with his finger. He said, quick and low, "Careful, James. You can't trust him."

Tom turned his head and saw Simon Watkins coming round the corner of the big barn, slapping his hands together as if to shake the dust off them. "That's done, Jack Jacobs," he boomed in his big voice. "Enough potatoes to set you up for the winter, all sorted nice and tidy at the end of the hayloft. I've seen Mrs. Mary about the side of pork she had ready for Mrs. Williams and made arrangements about the boar coming to service the sow, so I'll be off, no time like the present and no rest for the wicked, and thanks for the cider."

He ruffled Tom's hair with his bony hand. "And you make the most of it, lad," he said. "Bit of freedom."

Jack Jacobs said, "You've not seen Thomas before, so James says. He's my second son's oldest boy, lives up in the hills, come to spend a bit of time with his grandad."

Simon Watkins laughed. Jack Jacobs went on stroking his nose with the stem of his pipe. Gandy was silent. Simon Watkins said, "Just as you say, squire. Middle name is Discreet, as you know."

"I do know, Mr. Watkins," Jack Jacobs said gravely. "The best Newsbearer we've got."

"That's right," Simon Watkins bellowed, "that's the ticket. It's not work if you enjoy it, that's what I always say, and it was an added pleasure to have the chance of a good chinwag with your brother here. He's got a different viewpoint, you might say, looking at things from another angle than the one we're all stuck with. And interesting to be reminded of a bit of old history, what went on in the old days. Oh, indeedy. Indeed, to goodness, Mr. James Jacobs told me quite a few tales about some of the folk around here that surprised me."

"Oh, he would," Jack Jacobs said. "Shouldn't rely on him, though. My brother's always been one to get things upside down, inside out. A bit of a moron. A sandwich or two short of a picnic. Of course he's not been round these parts for a good while, so even if he were a lot smarter he'd be getting things wrong. Natural he should get Thomas mixed up with my Tommy. It's a family name, so I daresay that confused him. We'll straighten him out in a day or two, poor old fellow."

Tom was so angry! He said, "That's not fair. You're horrible, calling Gandy a moron! It's a lie, and it's *rude*. Everyone knows Gandy is *brilliant*. He's—"

"That's enough, Thomas," Jack Jacobs said. "Behave yourself. Speak when you're spoken to."

His eyes, gray like Gandy's, were cold as stone, but Tom wasn't afraid. In fact, he was even angrier. How dare this useless old man, this *Oldie,* speak to him so roughly! He bunched his fists and would have shouted back if Lizzie had not kicked him sharply on his ankle-bone. As he bent to rub it she hissed, "Shut up, daftie. You mustn't speak to a grown-up like that."

He was so astonished, he forgot how much his ankle hurt. He stared at her, open-mouthed.

He heard Jack Jacobs say, "I'll see you to the cart, Mr. Watkins. There's a message I'd like you to pass on if you're going up the Bank. And another if you're likely to pass by old Mrs. Evans. She's been poorly and our Mary will be up to see her later this evening. Before dark, of course."

Tom glowered after him. When Jack and Simon Watkins had turned the corner of the barn, he said, to Lizzie, "What did you do that for?"

"To shut you up, lad," Gandy said. "Jack had his reasons for saying what he did, and I daresay he'll tell us. I don't mind being called a half-wit if it gets us all out of trouble. And I think you'll find the pecking order is a bit different here from at home. So mind your manners, speaking to older folk. Won't hurt you, and you'll fit in a bit easier."

Lizzie said, "He *roared* at my *Grandad!*"

She sounded awed, almost afraid, as if Tom had done something quite extraordinary.

Gandy said, "He won't do it again, Liz, he's a quick learner. Do me a favor now, would you, and fetch me another mug of that extremely good cider."

"Of course, Great-Uncle, with pleasure." Lizzie made a little bob, a kind of curtsy, and disappeared into the house.

Gandy said, "What I recommend, is that you keep quiet and listen. That's what I aim to do. Best way of learning. That's a sensible girl. She'll put you right when you put a foot or two wrong. Meantime, here's Jack coming back, so lie low."

He looked beyond Tom, at his brother. He said, "Sorry about that, Jack. Watkins seemed an agreeable fellow, not someone I'd want to spend the rest of my life with, but he was giving us a lift and I thought it was only polite. Besides, once I got going, the old times came back, and I found myself running on."

Jack said, "Forget it. What's done is done. Just remember that not everyone is reliable on the Outside. That particular Postman and Newsbearer is more of a Talebearer."

He looked at Tom, smiling, and Tom expected him to apologize for shouting at him so abruptly and rudely. But all Jack said was, "Almost time for supper, young Tom. You better get off and under the pump if you're to be ready." And, as Lizzie appeared with the cider for Gandy, he added, "I daresay Liz here could do with some help with the little ones, so make yourself useful."

He stopped and appeared to be waiting for Tom to say something. Lizzie dug Tom in the ribs and whispered, "Say yes. And say *Great-Uncle Jack*."

Tom said, "Yes, Great-Uncle Jack."

Lizzie said, "They're all in the orchard with Mother. Come along, Cousin Tom."

She led him away, round the side of the house. She said, "Mother's my mother. And she's your Aunt Mary. You have to give grown-ups their proper titles or it isn't respectful. My grandfather is very particular about children being good-mannered."

Tom said nothing. Sometime soon he might have a chance to explain to Lizzie that where he came from it was old people who were respectful to children and not the other way round, but just at the moment it seemed best to keep silent. Besides, once round the house she was hurrying on, down a path through a garden where vegetables were growing, a blur of green either side of him, and he had to run to keep up with her. He could hear shouting and laughter and the next minute, Lizzie had opened a white gate into what he supposed was "the orchard"—at least, there were a lot of trees, some of them covered with apples—and there were the "little ones," a noisy crowd of children, all ages, running round, playing tag, throwing balls, fighting for their turn on the swings tied to the apple trees, shouting and screaming—a dreadful noise.

Tom put his hands over his ears. He said, "Can't you stop them?"

"Not short of drowning," Lizzie said, with what sounded like fair disgust.

"Are they all your . . ." Tom swallowed hard and forced himself. "Your brothers and sisters?"

Saying these rude words aloud made him dizzy with fear. But it was also rather exciting. He tried again. "You've got an awful lot of brothers and sisters."

"Five belong to Aunt Polly. She's my mother's sister. She and Uncle Ted live here too. Only six of these kids are my family."

She heaved a sudden, huge sigh. "And that's six too many."

She clapped her hands and yelled, in a voice almost as loud as Simon Watkins's, "Time for supper, under the pump first, hands and faces, get along sharpish."

She said, to Tom, "You grab a baby—that one

there, Joshua. I'll take the fat twins—the others just have to be pushed and prodded."

Tom didn't care to tell her he had never held a baby before. Joshua had a round, dirty face, and round blue eyes with black lashes. He gave Tom a serious, measuring look, and held out his arms. Tom picked him up, and found him surprisingly heavy. Lizzie said, "Don't hold him out in front of you like that, as if he was a bomb. He won't explode. Sit him on your hip."

She had an identical baby straddled either side of her, and Tom found that Joshua settled on his hip in the same way, quite naturally. It was a strange feeling, but not uncomfortable. As he followed Lizzie, merging with the stream of jostling children, he tried bouncing the boy, just a little, up and down, holding him tight and safe behind, until he squealed with pleasure and began bouncing himself and laughing wildly. Tom whispered to him, daringly, "I wouldn't mind someone like you for a little brother." And then, because Joshua was too young to laugh at him, "What did she mean, *under the pump?*"

They were round the front of the house again and the children were crowding round an upright object with a long handle. One of the bigger boys seized it, worked it up and down, and a stream of water shot out of a nozzle. One by one the children put their hands under the water, then their heads, very quickly, sluicing it over them, and dodging out, wet and giggling and shaking their hair back.

Still bouncing Joshua on his hip, Tom stood beside Lizzie. He said, "Don't you have a bathroom?"

"We don't use it," Lizzie said. "Waste of electricity. You need the generator to get the water uphill from the brook. So we use the well and the pump. Sometimes we're allowed to use the lavatory at night."

Tom snorted with laughter. Lizzie stared at him.

He spluttered, "What d'you do in the daytime? Or don't you ever need to go?"

"The babies have their potties," Lizzie said. "There's a privy down the bottom of the vegetable garden, for the rest of us. An earth closet. But of course we can't go there at night."

She spoke in such a matter-of-fact way that it was a minute before Tom thought to say, "Why not?"

She looked at him, her dark brows drawn together and her eyes puzzled. She said, "Don't you know? Everyone stays indoors at night. We're not allowed out much in the evenings, and never after dark."

Chapter 6

From the way they were all looking at him, he might have four eyes and green hair . . .

Tom had never sat at such a crowded table. It was long and narrow and made of some kind of dark, shiny wood. The children sat either side, squashed together on long, slippery benches. Great-Uncle Jack sat at one end with Gandy beside him, both in high-backed chairs, and Aunt Mary, Aunt Polly, and Uncle Ted sat at the other. Aunt Mary looked like Lizzie, except that her dark hair was shorter and turning gray, and Aunt Polly and Uncle Ted were both cheerful-looking people with round, firm-fleshed faces, Aunt Polly with a lot of frizzy red hair, and Uncle Ted with none. Tom found it hard not to stare and stare at his shiny pink head. He had never seen a really bald person before. Why didn't he wear a wig?

There were so many questions, Tom thought. Where was Lizzie's father? And Great-Uncle Jack's wife? And—more important at the moment—what was for supper?

Bowls of steaming vegetables were arranged down the middle of the table and Aunt Mary set down an enormous piece of meat on a sizzling platter in front of Jack Jacobs who got to his feet, long sharp knife in one hand, long-pronged fork in another. Tom looked at him nervously. He had never eaten meat but he knew there was no way he could refuse it. Just the thought of saying "no thank you" to Great-Uncle Jack made him turn cold and shiver. Besides, the smell was delicious. And he was hungry.

"Should cut well, Father," Aunt Mary said. She smiled up the long table at Great-Uncle Jack and at Gandy. "I hope you have a good appetite, Uncle James. You'll not have tasted pork like this in a good long while, I imagine."

"I never thought I would again," Gandy said. He put his hand in his pocket. "There wasn't much to bring you, not that I could conceal about my person, anyway, but I thought these might come in useful."

He held up a tiny packet that Tom recognized instantly, and handed it to the child seated next to him to pass down the line to Aunt Mary. When it reached her, she held it between thumb and finger, closed her eyes and said, "Let me guess."

Tom could tell from her little smile that she was playing a game; she had known what the packet must hold before she took it and felt it. And he was right. She opened her eyes and said, "I knew, soon as I saw the blue paper. My mother had a packet she'd brought with her when she left and even when she'd lost or broken most of them she kept the rest in the paper. I remember, when I was little, her showing me the one or two she had left, kept in a special place, in a tiny drawer in a desk, and I liked the blue paper, it felt so soft and so delicate . . ."

She looked at Gandy. "Oh, Uncle James, I'm so grateful. I'll keep one or two for myself and share out the others."

Aunt Polly said, "It's a long time since I've had a really good needle to work with. First thing I do with mine will be to make you a shirt, Uncle James."

Tom felt his head spin. All this *Uncle* and *Aunt* stuff was making him dizzy. He would never remember. And all this fuss over *needles* . . .

As if he knew what Tom was thinking, Jack Jacobs said, "Some things are hard to find hereabouts, Tom. Steel is one. There are a lot of things you can make do without but it's hard to sew a fine seam without the right implement. Or carve meat. This knife goes back a long way. I brought it with me when I left. I hope you like pork."

All the time he was talking, he was carving the meat: thick, pink slices, curling away from the thin, shining blade.

Tom looked at Gandy. Gandy said, "Boy needs to find out, Jack. This'll be his first chance to taste it."

The heads of all the older children at the table turned to look at Tom with amazement. As if he were some kind of alien.

One of the boys said, in a puzzled voice, "He's very *fat* for a starving person."

Gandy said, "People don't starve if they don't eat meat. And once Tom's run around with you lot for a week or so, he'll be as skinny as you are."

He winked at Tom and passed him a plate with a slice of pork on it. Everyone fell silent as Tom picked up his knife and fork. He looked at his plate to avoid their astonished eyes and felt his ears grow hot. But the smell of the meat seemed to be making him hungrier. He cut a small piece and put it in his mouth. It was tender, juicy, and melting, a little like savory gelatin. He thought he quite liked it.

He said, "It's okay. I mean, no big deal, but all right."

Someone gave him spoonfuls of potatoes and carrots and beans and cauliflower and applesauce, but he didn't look up until the clatter and chatter of plates and knives and forks and voices—children's voices, grown-up voices, burbles and squeaks from the babies—told him it was safe. He raised his head cautiously. The only person watching him now was Lizzie, sitting next to him, looking sidelong and sympathetic.

She whispered, "If you really and truly do hate it, you can put it on my plate. The kids won't notice, too busy stuffing their faces, they often shovel food between them anyway. The only grown-up who matters is Grandfather, and he's busy talking."

"But I do like it. Honestly. Thanks all the same."

In fact, Tom thought he would have liked another slice. But he wasn't sure what the rules were. At home, Penny would have watched his plate and offered him a second helping the moment it was empty. But then, at home, he would have been the most important person at the table, telling William and Penny and Gandy what he had been learning at school that day, what excursions he had been on, what he had seen in the Dome of Discovery, and they would have listened. Here, except for feeding the babies, the adults seemed to pay the children no attention at all. Gandy and Jack Jacobs were talking to each other, and Aunt Mary and Aunt Polly were laughing fit to bust at something Uncle Ted had just said.

Tom watched and listened as Gandy had told him to. Aunt Mary shouted up the table to Gandy, "What was the gossip from Mr. Discreet Watkins? Could you make any sense of it? I mean, anything about anyone you remembered?"

"Emlyn's dead, for one thing. My old friend, Emlyn Davies. Just a boy to me still, of course, so that was a shock. But Harriet's still going strong, I was glad to hear. Never married, so old Watkins told me."

Tom saw Gandy blush. And Jack Jacobs cackled with laughter and dug him in the ribs with his elbow. "Think she's still carrying a torch for you, do you Jamie? Fancy your chances?"

Gandy turned even redder and Tom was disgusted. It was unnatural to hear old people talk in this way. As if they were still interested in love and sex when everyone knew that sort of thing stopped when you were about forty. He felt sorry for Gandy, being embarrassed in this way by his brother.

But Gandy was laughing. He said, "You never know, do you? I just might get lucky."

He caught Tom's eye and looked away.

Aunt Mary said, "Father always said you were a bright spark, Uncle James. Too independent to hang on Inside. He's been expecting you a long time."

"I've been waiting," Gandy said. "You're rich in your grandchildren, James. I only have one. That made it hard to leave. Then the letter came with my marching orders and I had no choice."

The five grown-ups fell silent. They looked at each other with grave expressions. Jack Jacobs gave a heavy sigh and touched Gandy's shoulder. He said, "Later, I think. We'll talk later. Meanwhile, I believe Mary has made one of her good apple pies."

Tom was surprised and disappointed that no one had been offered a second helping of meat, but the apple pie made up for it. It was the best he had ever tasted, lovely crisp pastry and slushy apples inside, a bit sweet, a bit sour. Aunt Mary served the adults, and a bowl of thick, crusty, yellow cream was passed down the table for the children to help themselves. Tom took four huge spoonfuls and passed the almost empty bowl to Lizzie, who said, "You might leave a titchy scrap for other people."

He saw his own plate piled high and said, ashamed, "I'm sorry, I'm not used . . . I mean, at home, there's just me."

"Lucky pig," she said crossly. "I mean, you're lucky *and* you're a pig."

"I've never *tasted* this stuff before. What we call cream is quite different. Not nearly so nice. If this is what you get to eat all the time then I think that *you're* lucky."

"No quarreling. Not at the table."

That was Uncle Ted, frowning at them, bald head bent forward and gleaming.

Cheek, Tom thought. Uncle Ted hadn't said a word to him up to now. It was unfair to start by telling him off!

But Lizzie said, "Sorry, Uncle Ted. It wasn't really a quarrel. He took more than his share but that was just a mistake. He's an only child. He doesn't have any brothers and sisters."

Heads turned again, ten pairs of eyes fixed on Tom. Even the babies seemed to regard him with wonder as if he were something they had never seen before, an exotic creature from another world beyond their imagining. Well, he *was* from another world, in a way, Tom thought irritably, but from the way they were all looking at him he might have four eyes and green hair and a horn sticking out of each ear.

Jack Jacobs rapped on the table with his spoon. "Eat up your pie, all of you," he commanded and ten pairs of eyes switched from Tom to their plates.

Aunt Mary said, "When you have both finished, Lizzie, you may take Tom with you to collect the eggs and shut up the chickens. Show him around while it's light."

Tom settled to his apple pie and his mountain of cream without looking up. He tried to pretend he was invisible. If he couldn't see the other children, they couldn't see him. The trouble was he could hear them: mutters and giggles and coughs and snuffles and damp, champing sounds of eating. He thought longingly about his room at home. It was small but he was alone there. No eyes watching him.

He scraped his plate clean and glanced sideways at Lizzie. She nodded, swung her legs neatly round and over the bench and stood up. He tried to copy her, caught his foot, and nearly fell, which made some of the smaller children laugh.

Lizzie took his hand. "Come on," she said. "*Ignore.*" And as she led him out of the big farm kitchen, "Kids, I hate them!"

She picked up a wooden trug in the porch and handed it to him. "Eggs," she said, marching off ahead, through the green gate in the stone wall, wheeling sharp right and ducking through a gap in a straggly hedge. Tom followed her, into a big green space that sloped gently down to a line of trees. "Chicken field," she told him. "That is, it's where the buggers ought to be. We'll look in the nesting boxes, just in case one of them has obliged, then we start the real hunt. Okay?"

"Okay," Tom said meekly. He had thought chickens lived in cages, eating from a trough at one end and dropping their eggs at the other. Here it seemed they roamed free, scratching and strutting around until they were shut up at night in the hen-house.

"Chck, chck, chck," Lizzie sang softly, taking a handful of grain from her pocket, and the brown chickens ran to her, necks stretched, wings lifted a little away from their bodies. They gathered around her, pecking and chuckling, following her to the ramp that led into their house. "Ready for bed," Lizzie said. "Nighty-night, don't let the foxes bite."

Her voice was lovingly soft. Tom said, "D'you like chickens better than people?"

She tossed her head and laughed. "I just wish *I* was an only child."

And she ran off down the slope to the trees. When Tom caught up with her she was on her knees beside a brook, feeling under a scrubby bush on the bank. "Thought so," she said, holding up an egg in each hand. "That's the sort of place to look. Hedges and bushes and ditches, some-times places you wouldn't think, like there's one old hen always lays round the back of the privy."

She put the eggs in Tom's trug. "Have a look inside that old tree if you like. We had a broody hen hatched out ten chicks there last spring. She stopped laying after that, so we ate her."

The hollow oak smelled sinister to Tom: an ancient, wet, rotten smell. If Lizzie had not been there, he would not have dared peer inside. Old, hollow trees were known to be especially dangerous because spiteful spirits often made their homes there. He held his breath, partly because of the smell, partly from terror. And there, at the back of the hollow, was a nest made of leaves and bits of twig, and in the nest, one large white egg, covered with freckles.

He backed out from the hollow, carefully holding the egg. He said, "It's warm." He knew that must mean it had only just been laid by the hen but it seemed to him like a marvel. He said, "I've never touched a really new egg before."

Lizzie looked at him with the little frown he was getting used to. He said, "I'm used to buying eggs in boxes. It's no odder than scrabbling about under bushes."

Lizzie said, "If I had my way, I'd keep the hens shut up in the barn. Safe from the foxes, and we could collect the eggs quicker. But my mother says this way is best. A broody hen can sit on her eggs in a nice quiet place and hatch out healthy chicks with no trouble to anyone."

"I don't think hunting eggs is a trouble," Tom said.

In fact, half an hour or so later, he realized he was enjoying himself. On the other side of the bridge, there was a little wood, and beyond that, a ditch and a high hedge that marked the boundary of the farm. Keeping it safe, like the wall round an Urb, Tom decided, and was glad to find something about this strange place on the Outside that matched up with something familiar.

But he didn't tell Lizzie this. He was too busy searching for eggs and each one he found was a prize. "It's like a treasure hunt," he said, when the trug was full of eggs, brown eggs and white eggs and speckled eggs.

Lizzie said, "It's getting dark, we'd best go in," and he saw the sun had almost gone; all that was left was a white blaze on the edge of the hill behind the house, and the moon had risen in a pale, clear, greenish sky.

"Not dark yet," he said. He realized, suddenly, that he was feeling not only happy but *safe,* not just in the chicken field but in the wood on the other side of the brook. If there were tree-spirits here, they were friendly and meant him no harm. And there were good smells: grassy smells, sweet, evening air smells, instead of the child-smells and cooking smells of the house. He said, "It's nice here. Can't we stay a bit longer?"

Lizzie said, quite snappily, "I don't want to go in either. There's nothing to do in the evenings. I've read all the books we've got and Talebearer Watkins only does the book exchange round once every six weeks. But there'll be a silly fuss if we're out after sundown and it'll be me in trouble, not you."

She started to hurry up the slope to the house that stood at the top of the rise. In the windows that looked on the chicken field, Tom could see lamps shining yellow.

He caught up with Lizzie and panted, "I don't see. Why the hurry?"

"Rules," Lizzie said. "This one is because of the Dropouts. No one minds a few eggs or apples but some of them have turned nastier lately."

"I don't understand—" Tom began, and she turned on him angrily.

"You don't understand *anything*, do you?"

"I do," Tom said, equally angry. "I understand a lot of things *you* don't seem to know about. You don't even have television . . ."

"Oh, shut *up*," she said. "You're as bad as grandmother. She—"

"Lizzie. Tom." Aunt Mary stood at the top of

the chicken field. The dusk was falling fast now and her white apron gleamed bright. "Come along in," she called. "Grandmother is asking for you. She wants to see Tom. Quick sharp now."

Chapter 7

"Someone new to moan at . . ."

"I thought she must have gone away," Tom whispered, as they took the eggs into the dairy. This was a long, cool, white room off the kitchen, with a stone floor and a sweet, milky smell.

"She stays in bed," Lizzie said. "My mother says she's ill. Grandfather says she's ill. There's an old doctor who comes sometimes and *he* says she must be ill or she wouldn't stay in bed."

She put the wooden trug on a marble slab and tossed her head. "Come on," she said. "Get it over and done with."

The big kitchen was empty now, the table bare, everything tidy. A low red fire glowed in a black grate. After the cool of the dairy this room seemed very hot. Tom said, "Why d'you have a fire in summer?"

"Cooking, of course," Lizzie said. "That's an old range oven. It had been bricked up—oh, years and years, when Grandfather came and un-bricked it. My mother says it's a good cooker, she likes it, but she'd say anything to please Grandfather."

She opened the door of the kitchen. Tom followed her into a dark hall, stone-flagged like the kitchen and dairy, with several heavy-looking closed doors and a staircase of dark, polished wood leading up. The banister rail was polished, smooth and slippery to the hand, and there were little oaken owls carved on the newel posts. Up a flight of stairs, there was a long corridor, with more doors, and a long window with a cushioned seat under it. Outside the window, the trees stood black against the last of the light.

"The brats are on the next floor," Lizzie said. "Up that cupboard stair, in the attics. You're down here with the grown-ups, sharing with Great-Uncle James." She sniffed with contempt. "In case poor little boy wakes in the night and gets lonely!"

Tom thought, *I could have a really good quarrel with this needling girl*. But he decided against it. He said, in a mock-humble voice, "I might get *very* scared, you're quite right. It's such a huge house, isn't it?"

She looked disappointed. "Oh, I don't know. There's a lot of us living here. And other kids hereabouts come to Aunt Polly's school in the big room downstairs. Kids from the White House, and The Roveries, and the Bent Hill Farm. Most homesteads are big old places. Some of them have got several families sharing."

Tom couldn't think what to say to this, so he said nothing, though it seemed strange to him, more than one family in the same living unit. Instead, he said, "Who lived here before? I mean long ago. Before Great-Uncle Jack came and unbricked the oven?" He remembered what Gandy had told him. "Was it *his* uncle?"

"I don't know if *that* old Uncle was still alive when Grandfather came. If you want *history*, you have to ask Aunt Poll."

They had walked the length of the corridor, on polished boards gleaming like satin. A door stood a little ajar, a line of light shining. Lizzie pushed the door and it swung fully open. She said, "Here he is, Grandmother."

She lay in bed, propped up on white pillows, white covers over her, a white lace shawl round her shoulders. There was a pile of books on the table beside her and a table lamp with a flame in its glass funnel. Its yellow light lit the bed and the woman in it, leaving the corners of the room in soft shadow.

She held out her hand and said, "Come here,

Tom. Let me look at you. And take a good look at me while you're about it, if you can bear another relation."

She didn't sound old or ill. And she didn't look it. Her voice was strong, her eyes were clear, and her cheeks a good, healthy pink. Only her hands were an invalid's hands, pale and delicate-looking and soft to the touch.

She held Tom's hand between both of hers. She said, "Thomas Jacobs. My great-nephew. I'm your great-aunt. Tess Smith, that was my name before I married Jack Jacobs, but the way they go on here, with Aunt-this and Grandmother-that, I'm sometimes afraid I'll forget it. But you may call me Tess, if you will. And I'll call you Tom. Is that a bargain?"

"I suppose so. If you like," he said slowly. He was conscious of Lizzie behind him. In his mind, he saw her little owl's nose wrinkling up, sneering at him. Though why should he mind her? He said, "All right, Tess. I don't mind if you don't."

"It'll upset Grandad," Lizzie said. "*She* knows that."

Tess didn't answer her. She patted the side of the bed and said, "Now, Tom. You tell me what's going on back home. On the Inside. Do you still have television?"

Lizzie groaned. Tess said, "No interruptions

from you, Granddaughter. Stay if you like but keep quiet and maybe you'll learn something." She sighed and smiled at Tom. "Oh, I do miss it," she said. "But I expect it's changed since I was your age. I used to watch *Neighbours* and *Baywatch*. And videos. Oh, Thomas Jacobs! I'd give my soul for a video."

Sitting on the edge of the bed, Tom could see Lizzie now. Her face was stern and her eyes were bright. Their color seemed to change all the time; in the yellow lamplight they looked tawny. He said, watching Lizzie, "It depends what's beamed in to the Screen. The schedule's drawn up by the Guardians and okayed by the Protectors. There's a lot of science on the Cosmic Web. And at the weekend we mostly get virtual reality films of the olden days. Knights in armor on horseback, or wars in the last century. People killing each other."

"You mean, you can't *choose* what to watch?"

Tom said, puzzled, "You can turn the Screen off. Is that what you mean? But they know if you do that. Through the monitors."

Tess said, "We used to have lots of channels. Soaps and chat shows and lovely old films. You could watch twenty-four hours of the day if you wanted to. That wouldn't do here, of course. It's *work for the night cometh* here on the Outside."

She clutched at Tom's hand. "I should never

have come, Tom. *You'll have a hard row to hoe—* that's what my parents said. *Look at the company you'll be keeping. Criminals and layabouts and all the no-hopers.* I said my Jack was different and *they* said his brother James was staying behind so that was no argument. They said Jack hadn't asked me to come and that made my mind up. They locked me in my room and I climbed out of the window . . ."

Tom said, "Gandy told me he only stayed because he had to look after his wife and his baby. That was my father. The baby, I mean." He felt helpless suddenly. He said, "I don't really know what happened, anyway. Except what I've been told. That things had got bad in the cities, nothing worked anymore, people were hungry most of the time, and afraid all the time. There were no jobs and no money. So the Protectors told the Guardians to get rid of the dangerous elements in the cities, the thieves and the muggers, and then they built the Wall to keep the good people all safe inside."

He wondered if he should tell Tess about the other things he'd been told, about the barbarians in the Wild who caught and ate children, but decided against it. Not with Lizzie standing there in the shadows, her tawny eyes scornful.

Tess said, "Safe! *Safe!* That's a lovely word,

Tom. Don't let them make you despise it here. You might think a poor, sick old woman like me had a right to feel safe, wouldn't you? Oh, I should have listened to my parents, not gone chasing after Jack without knowing what it would lead to. Lying here every night, sick to my heart with fear . . ."

Lizzie said, impatiently, "*Grandmother!* The homestead is safe. Bolted and barred after dark."

"Oh, you know it all, don't you? Miss Sharp-Tongue!"

Tess gave a deep sigh, and leaned back against her white pillow. In spite of her pink cheeks, she looked very frail suddenly. Tom said, "I'm sorry you're so ill. It must be dull, having to stay in bed all the time."

She looked at him suspiciously, gathering herself to be angry. But when she saw he had spoken quite innocently she smiled at him sadly. "I don't mind being dull, Tom. That's the least of the crosses I have to bear. I'm in no pain, it's just this terrible weakness. It comes from working so hard for so many years, out in the fields all weathers . . ."

Lizzie gave one of her sniffs, a small sound but Tom heard it, and Tess must have heard it too because she said, rather quickly, "The worst thing is knowing what a trouble I am to everyone, but what can I do? Sometimes I think it would be a mercy if I were released from this unhappy world, and not just a mercy for me . . ."

"If you go on like that, I'll tell Grandfather," Lizzie said in an ominous voice.

Tess laughed. "Oh, no, you won't, Granddaughter. He doesn't like tittle-tattles. And you wouldn't want to upset him anyway. It's just, seeing a new pair of eyes, I see myself in them. A useless old woman, cluttering up the place, nothing to do except go back over the past and see where I went wrong."

Lizzie said, sounding suddenly kinder, "You're not useless, Grandmother. You're the only one tells us what it was like before. When everyone lived on the Inside. About television and telephones and motor cars and dishwashers, stuff like that. I mean, Grandfather must know but he won't talk about it. And you're only weak because you lie in bed all the time. If you'd get up and walk, just round the room, just for a little while, you'd start to feel better."

Gandy said, from the doorway, "Child's right, Tess. Nothing wrong with your legs, is there? Pretty legs, I seem to remember."

"Oh, James . . ."

Tess's bright blue eyes filled with tears. She put out her hand and Gandy came to her bedside and took it. She said, "I don't think they'd carry me very far now. Not where I want to go, anyway."

"Nobody's legs will take them back to the past," Gandy said. "And if you mean what I think you mean, Tess my darling, you'd find everything very much altered. Not to your liking at all, believe me."

He smiled as he spoke but his gray eyes had darkened. Watching him, Tom wondered how old Tess was. Jack was younger than Gandy but Tess might not be. She could even be the same age as Gandy. Old enough for the Letter to come!

It made him feel dizzy. He stood up and moved away from the bed and felt for Lizzie's warm hand. She whispered, "She'll be all right now." And then, aloud, "Good night, Grandmother."

Tom echoed, "Good night," but the old woman in the bed only waved a pale hand in dismissal. She was too busy smiling at Gandy.

"She likes someone new to moan at," Lizzie said. "If Great-Uncle James hadn't come, you'd have been stuck there for hours."

Tom thought he wouldn't have minded; he had rather liked Tess. He said so. He added, "All the other grown-ups sort of *bark* at you here. And expect you to jump when they say so. At home, I mean, on the Inside, children are—well—much more *important*. Old people don't matter. And when they get *very* old, so they can't any longer do anything . . ."

He looked at her. He said, "What's wrong with Tess? She doesn't look ill. Not the least little bit."

She shrugged her shoulders. "How should I know? Mother says, sometimes old people take to their beds. As if they feel they've done enough of the world's work and fancy a rest. Mother says, why shouldn't they, if that's how they feel? They looked after the rest of us long enough. It's their turn to lie easy."

This was a surprising idea to Tom. He turned it over in his mind. He said, "But that's awfully expensive, isn't it? What they call uneconomic?"

She looked at him, dark brows knitted together. She started rubbing the side of her small owlish nose just as Gandy did sometimes, when he was thinking. She said, "I don't know what you mean. There she is, Tess Jacobs who wishes she was still Tess Smith! What else could we do except take care of her? Got any ideas, Mr. Clever-Dick-Tom?"

She looked so smug, so superior! To wipe that look off her face Tom told her about Gandy's Letter. About Nostalgia Block 95. And the Memory Theme Park. It made him feel cold all over, and sick. Somehow, putting it into words was worse than just knowing it and keeping it locked tight inside. He said, dry-mouthed, "I'm sorry. It's awful. I shouldn't have told you."

But—and in a way, he thought later, this was

much worse—she just *smiled!* Smiled and smiled. And then said, "Well, it's what she wants, isn't it? Tess. She keeps saying so. Why don't you tell her how she can get it?"

Chapter 8

"Fancy Mars Bars going out of fashion!"

And Gandy had told her. He said to Tom, when they were both in bed, lying in the dark with the window wide and the scents of the summer night drifting in, "I think you may find your Great-Aunt Tess up and about in a day or so. Making the best of a bad job, that's how she'll put it."

Tom said, "She's not really ill, then?"

"I wouldn't think so. Mind you, I don't know. But she always liked her comforts, did Tess. That's why Jack went Outside without her. That, and her being older than he is. He was afraid it would turn out too hard for her. And maybe it has been. But she always had a lot of *go* to her. Liked her own way. So we'll see."

Tom said, "She's decided not to go back Inside

then? I suppose she thought there wasn't much future in it!"

Gandy chuckled. Then he turned the chuckle into a cough. He said, severely, "That's not funny, Tomkins."

Tom hadn't thought it was funny. Just a black joke, the kind that made you laugh and shudder at the same time. He said quickly, "Change the subject, Gandy. I wish we'd brought William and Penny with us." An uncomfortable thought, one he hadn't wanted to think, but that had been nagging at the back of his mind, formed itself into words. He said, reluctantly, "They'll be all right, won't they? William and Penny?" He thought, *my mother, my father*. Lizzie would think him very peculiar if she heard him calling his parents by their first names. He said, "I mean, they won't get into trouble?"

"Because they didn't deliver me up when they should have done? Don't worry, Tom. The computer at Nostalgia Block 95 will have gone down by the time I should have arrived there. The Trusty on duty will have to make a written report. He'll enter James Makepeace Jacobs in the manifest, but without the usual DNA checking. The Protectors won't question it. Those computers are always breaking down. And, look at it from their point of view, it's not really important if a few of us have cut loose. Gone under the wire, off the road. As long as they get rid of us, one way or the other."

Tom said, in a tight voice, "It's hard to get used to. The idea. What they do to the Oldies."

"Makes sense to the Protectors," Gandy said. "Most people just want a comfortable life. Enough jobs, enough food, enough fun. Enough to go round. Time you get to sixty-five, you've *had* enough, all you're entitled to, that's how they see it. Any more, and you're becoming a burden. You can't expect all us Oldies to agree with them, though. Hence the mysterious unreliability of the computer in the Nostalgia Block."

Tom lay stiff in his bed. Gandy sounded so certain. But he was an Oldie. Was he making it up? He said, "How did you know? I mean, how could you be sure?"

"About the computer? And the Trusty on duty? Word of mouth, Tom, like Simon Watkins the Postman and Talebearer. One mouth to another along a chain of what you call my funny old friends. We call it the Railway. Not every Trusty wants to make use of it, which is just as well, come to think of it. Might be difficult for the Protectors to turn a blind eye if there were too many taking that route. Difficult for the Rangers here likewise."

"A Ranger is a sort of Trusty?"

"More or less. The Rangers are more like our

Guardians, the lower rank of the Service. Not all that much to guard on the Outside but they keep their eyes open and do what has to be done round the country, and they patrol this side of the Wall. The Scouts oversee them, do most of the office work. Scouts are a bit like our Trusties, only there aren't so many of them. For one thing, computers make work and the Outside has no computers. It's all word of mouth again. And much simpler. You heard that Ranger, telling me to go into the Rangers' Office? That's all I have to do, show the letter to the Scout on duty, get the right stamp, and I'm legal. May be more of a fuss to get you accepted, we may have to go up a bit higher, to the Sheriffs' Assembly, so your Great-Uncle Jack thinks, but I don't anticipate any difficulty."

"Are the Sheriffs the High Ones? Like the Protectors?"

Tom tried the names in his mind. It was odd, he thought. *Protectors* was supposed to be a kind word, but in fact it was frightening.

Gandy said, "Oh, quite different. The Sheriffs are elected. Chosen, that is, one for each district. You won't know that because it doesn't happen Inside. Here, every two years, they have what they call an *election*. Everyone goes into the nearest Rangers' Office and casts a vote. That is, writes the name of the person they want to be the local Chief

Scout on a piece of paper and puts it in a box. And a Ranger counts the votes up and declares the winner."

Tom was silent. This was the strangest thing he had heard about the Outside so far. He could just about grasp their peculiar ideas about grown-ups being more important that children. If every family had lots of children, each child would not be so special. And he believed now that trees were not as dangerous as he had been told—that had been a story to stop people escaping off the road into the Wild. But the thought that ordinary people might actually choose the High Ones, the Masters, was absurd, fantastic. Unbelievable. He said, "But they might choose the wrong person!"

Gandy laughed and yawned at the same time. "Indeed they might, Tomkins."

He was sounding, suddenly, very sleepy. Tom said, quickly, "Is it only the Trusties who can get out on the Railway? What happens to other people who might want to go? Like teachers or doctors or Guardians. Or William and Penny?"

Gandy said, "Is it right that a few lucky ones can get away? Or should they stay and go down with the others? It's an old argument, Tom. And not one I'm up to just now. I'm sorry . . ."

His voice trailed away. Tom said, "What did you mean, not every Trusty wants to make use of the Railway? Why not? Why don't they?"

No answer. Gandy had fallen asleep, flat on his back; by the light of the moon flooding in through the window, Tom could see his black beard pointing to the ceiling.

Tom closed his own eyes but although he was tired, his mind was racing. So much had happened in such a short time. He could hardly believe that only this morning he had been so ignorant about what lay beyond the Wall. In the Wild. Gandy had called it "the real world." He had also said it was dangerous.

It didn't seem dangerous, Tom thought, lying in his narrow but comfortable bed in this quiet house, with Gandy snorting and snuffling in a bigger bed no more than an arm's length away. He could poke him easily if he wanted to stop him snoring (which was what the snuffles and snorts were working up to) but he felt too lazy to budge.

Heavily tired, too, arms and legs aching. All that running about they seemed to go in for Outside! Gandy had said, if he did the same, he would be as skinny as Lizzie's brothers and sisters and cousins in no time. Tom had thought they were bony and horrible. Children were meant to be fat, as they all were on the Inside, with plump arms and legs and soft wide bottoms and dimples in their chins. If you were nice and fat, it showed you were properly fed and looked after. "You want to grow up a credit to all those who take care of you," the Nourishment Assistants said at school dinner-time, pressing them to eat another helping of potatoes, another piece of pie. Weighing them at the end of term and reminding them to keep up the good work in the holidays.

Tom thought it was lucky the holidays had only just begun. A whole eight weeks before the school would realize he'd gone, and start checking up on William and Penny.

He shifted in bed and the springs creaked, a loud *twang* in the still night. He worried in case the noise should wake Gandy. But while Gandy snuffled peacefully on, someone else was awake and stirring. Footsteps in the passage outside the room. Soft padding sounds, someone creeping . . .

He held his breath, sitting bolt upright, straining to listen. No more footsteps, nothing except the small moaning and groaning sounds of an old house at night. *Settling,* he thought, like the old dog downstairs, turning round in its basket. Then he heard something else. Someone sneezed. Outside the window . . .

Gandy was snoring properly now: a full orchestra of trumpets blaring. The bed shook with awesome vibrations; the window frame rattled. Tom bounced out of bed and ran to the open window.

The room was at the front of the house. As he

looked down on the strip of garden and the low stone wall, the kitchen door opened and someone came out: a small figure, hunched and ghostly in the moonlight, wearing a white lace shawl round her shoulders.

She was carrying a wide, flat basket, like the trug Lizzie had taken when they had collected the eggs, and there were eggs in it; Tom could see them shining. There were other things as well but they didn't reflect the moon's light like the eggs so Tom could only guess what they might be. He thought he saw a pale fawny shadow that could be a loaf of bread.

Tess opened the little gate and carried the trug across the yard. When she reached the pump, she set the trug down beside it and whistled—one clear, sweet note like a bird-call. Then she turned to come back to the house, looking up as she did so. Tom had no time to duck out of sight.

She laughed. She said, coming closer, beneath his window, "No wonder you can't sleep, Great-Nephew, with your Grandfather James making a noise like a foghorn. Enough to waken the dead. D'you know what a foghorn is? Never mind. You come down, keep me company. I have to wait here a while."

Tom was in his underpants. This was the first night of his life that his mother had not taken all his clothes to be sanitized when he went to bed, and laid a fresh sleeping robe on his pillow. There was a jug of water and a basin on a stand by the window. He poured a little water into the basin and splashed his face and rinsed his hands and armpits and dampened his hair, but as he pulled on yesterday's trousers and the scratchy shirt Gandy had stolen, he still felt unhygienic and smelly. He hoped Tess wouldn't notice. Perhaps, since they didn't seem to have a deodorizer, they were all used to each other's smells and didn't mind them.

He was anxious as he went downstairs. But once he had joined Tess, sitting on a wooden bench by the glowing range fire in the tidy kitchen, her lamp beside her on the table, he stopped worrying and felt comfortable with her. "Come here, Tom," she said. "Sit by me. That's right, nice and close. I feel the cold even on summer nights; I could do with someone young to warm up my bones."

It was surprisingly easy to snuggle up to her. And interesting to smell *her* smell which was flowery and powdery and dry.

He said, "What were you doing just now? Did you have eggs in that trug?"

"Other things too," she said. "A nice fresh loaf and some good fat slices of bacon and a piece of the cheese my Polly brought home from Bishop's Castle today. You'll not sneak on me, will you? It's out of order, what I do."

"I don't know what you *do* do, do I?" Tom said, and chuckled. "I thought your poor legs wouldn't carry you anywhere."

"Oh, they're strong enough when I need them," she said. "As for what I do, I keep faith." She looked at him with her bright blue eyes growing moist. She said it again. "I keep faith with my Charley."

This was even more mysterious. Maybe she was talking gibberish. Maybe she wasn't ill in her body as she pretended to be, but ill in her mind . . .

She said, "I take what I think won't be noticed whenever I can and leave it for the lost souls out there. The others call them the Dropouts. My boy is with them. Not a boy to your mind, of course, my boy's a grown man now, but he was my last child, some twelve years after Mary and Poll, and I remember him young. I don't suppose it's Charley who comes for the food, but whoever needs it is welcome. I go against Jack for Charley's sake."

She sighed and shook her head. Then she said, in a quite different voice, "You didn't bring a Mars Bar with you by any wonderful chance?"

"No," Tom said. "That is, I don't think so. What is a Mars Bar?"

She didn't answer him, just rolled her eyes to heaven and sighed again, so he went on, "Lizzie said, the Dropouts were bad. Turning nasty, she said."

Tess said, indignantly, "You'd turn nasty, Tom, if you were hungry and cold and knew other people were warm in their beds. My poor Charley! Jack was glad when he was born, a boy after two girls. The girls were too young to be married then, so he had no man to help on the farm. But Charley wasn't a work horse to be flogged to death. He was around fourteen when Jack began to bear down and be hard on him. Charley upped sticks and left. He'd be going on nineteen by now. It was after he went that I took sick in my bed."

She pushed Tom away from her and looked at him intently. "You're sure you don't know what a Mars Bar is? You're not holding out on me? Oh— of course not, why should you?" She giggled. "That's one more reason not to go back Inside! I'll have to make the best of a bad job and stay on. Who'd have thought Mars Bars would go out of fashion!"

She patted Tom's knee and stood up. "If you want to be helpful, young man, you can go and fetch that trug. It'll be empty by now. You can put it back in the dairy and no one will be any wiser. I think you'll agree, you've kept me up long enough with your gossiping. So just push the bolt when you come back and make sure you be quiet on the stairs."

She took her lamp with her. It was dark in the

big kitchen and Tom stumbled over the old dog, asleep in its basket. It lifted its head with a low, mumbly snarl but when Tom held out his hand to be sniffed, it licked him with a warm tongue, stretched its legs rigid, and then curled softly to sleep again.

Tom stood in the open door and looked out. The yard was drenched in moonlight. He could make out the shape of the trug by the pump. He thought it looked empty but he couldn't be sure. He didn't *have* to fetch it! He wasn't afraid, of course, he wasn't afraid! But it was none of his business! After all, he hadn't *said* he would do it!

He was walking out of the little gate in the stone wall, across the yard. The moonlight made the yard very white and the shadows very black. He tried not to look at them. Why should he be scared of an old Dropout? Might as well be afraid of a tree!

All the same, once he had picked up the empty trug he ran back to the house as fast as he could, heart thumping, cheeks jolting. And once inside he slammed the bolt hard and had to lean against the door for a while to get his breath back. His legs were still shaky even after he had put the trug safe in the dairy and crept up the stairs and along the passage toward the sound of Gandy's tumultuous snoring.

Surprising the whole house wasn't awake! But at least if they were, that astonishing din would drown any noise he was making.

He closed the door gently behind him and went to the window. Below him the yard lay pale and innocent under the moon. There was the barn, the pump, the roof of the pigsty, and the high hedge that flanked the deep lane beyond them.

Then something moved. A piece of shadow detached itself from the blackness of the hedge, moved into the light, and turned itself into a man. A man with a cap on his head, perched on his long, blond hair. He looked at Tom in the window and, fearfully, Tom began to shrink back. But then the man took off his cap, and in the full light of the moon, twirled it in front of him and bowed low.

Tom didn't see him go. He blinked—blinked once—and the man was gone.

Chapter 9

"What have you done? Where is Joshua?"

At first, when he woke in the morning, his mind still saw the man with the long blond hair twirling his cap and bowing before him. Then Gandy's voice broke in, and his clear picture of the night visitor turned transparent and ghostly until it floated away into mist. Like a dream . . .

Gandy said, "Up, boy. Up and doing. Your Great-Uncle Jack has plans for you this morning."

Tom yawned and scowled. He put his legs out of bed. He said, "What about my clothes? I can't put on these horrible, dirty things, not *again*. And I smell. You smell too, I expect."

But Gandy was looking very spruce. Although he was still in his old jeans, he was wearing a crisp-looking clean shirt. His black beard shone and his face was rosy.

He said, "I've been down to the brook. Cold but refreshing. You get a hot bath in the copper once a week here; the rest of the time it's the brook or the pump. And your Aunt Polly has looked out some clothes for you. We reckoned Uncle Ted's gear would do for now. You're tall for your age and he's short for his and you can roll up the legs of the pants if you need to."

"I don't want to wear someone else's clothes," Tom said crossly. "Not an old man's clothes, anyway."

"None of the kids are broad enough in the beam," Gandy said. "So want must be your master."

His cheerful tone startled Tom. He might have to get used to the other grown-ups on the Outside ordering him about rudely, but he didn't see why he should put up with it from Gandy. He said, "It's not my fault they're all so disgustingly *thin*. Bags of bones."

"Here it's thought to be healthier to be a fraction less fleshy," Gandy said, rather more kindly. "But I can see that may take some getting used to. So try Uncle Ted's gear, there's a good lad, and there may be some breakfast left if you hurry. Meals are on time in Owlbury Hall, and if you're late there's no snacking."

Uncle Ted's clothes fitted snugly and once the sleeves and the legs were rolled up, Tom found them comfortable, if a bit scratchy. The shirt had a fancy, flecky pattern woven into it that he liked, but it was without pockets. He discovered this when he was transferring things out of his dirty trousers, his penknife, his identity card, a chewed piece of gum he had screwed up in a handkerchief. And the key Gandy had given him.

He felt for his breast pocket. But that had been in his Wonderclean shirt. A pocket with a buttoned flap was a safer place to keep a key than stuffed with a lot of other junk in his trousers. The key was on a necklace of rolled leather, just long enough to squeeze over his head. A tight fit over his ears, doubling one of them over quite painfully, but he managed it and the key settled neatly at the base of his throat as if it belonged there. He buttoned the neck of his shirt over it. He thought he should hide it. He didn't know why.

Gandy had been right. Breakfast was almost over. Aunt Mary was clearing the table. There had been eggs, Tom noted, seeing the shells, but none left. "Early birds get fed best in this house," Aunt Mary said. "There's bread and a bit of good cheese, stick some in your pocket. Your Great-Uncle don't like being kept waiting."

There were a few little ones left at the table, all

strapped into chairs. As Tom cut his bread and cheese, one of them beat a spoon on the tray in front of him and let out a high, sharp cry. When Tom looked at him, Joshua held out his arms and screeched, his cheeks flooding with color.

"Give him a kiss before you go," Aunt Mary said. "He's taken to you, I can see, and that's a fair compliment. He's fussy, is Joshua."

A little shyly, Tom kissed Joshua's cheek. He liked his smell, milk and jam, perhaps a faint hint of pee, but that didn't seem too bad in a baby. Joshua grabbed his finger and wrapped his small hand around it, bouncing, with loud, urgent shrieks, up and down in his chair.

"He wants you to pick him up," Aunt Mary said. "But you've got to go. There'll be time to play with him this afternoon, when we're harvesting."

A shout from outside, "Get that idle boy moving, Mary," and she jerked her head toward the door. "Bark mostly worse than his bite, Tom, but I think you should jump to it. The alternative is Aunt Polly's school but your grandfather thought that might be too much your first morning."

Tom jumped to it. He didn't care to admit it, even to himself, but he was scared of Great-Uncle Jack. But when he dared to look up at him, he saw his gray eyes were smiling. He said, "Your grandfather wants me to explain what *he* calls our post-industrial society. Your grandfather is a clever man, too clever for me. All I can do is to see if you'd make a farmer."

"But I'm going to be a refuse disposal engineer," Tom said, without thinking. When Jack Jacobs raised his eyebrows, he tried to explain. "We get told what we're going to do. So everyone has a place. They use the computer to see how many people they'll need for each kind of work and when we're born they fit us all in."

Jack Jacobs said nothing. He was watching Tom with an odd expression on his face. Almost as if he were sorry for him.

Tom said, "A refuse disposal engineer has a very important position in the Urbs. When lots of people live close together there is a huge problem with waste."

"Ah!" Jack Jacobs said. "Yes. I would suppose so."

"Gandy—I mean, Grandfather, was a water engineer before he was made a Trusty. That's just as important."

His great-uncle nodded gravely. "And farming?"

Tom considered. He knew that he was supposed to believe everyone's job was of equal importance. But he found himself saying, "I think farming must be quite dull. You have to commute out of your Urb every morning. And you either have a barley farm, or a wheat farm, or you just grow potatoes. Or you have an egg factory. They're all factories, really. Nothing to do except look after the machinery."

Jack Jacobs said "Ah!" again. He was sucking an unlit pipe. He took it out of his mouth now and stroked his nose with the stem. Then he began, very slowly, to pack the bowl with tobacco from a leather pouch, tamping it down with his finger. But he didn't light it. He put it back in his pocket and said, abruptly, "We don't have much machinery on this homestead. No tractors. We use horses." Suddenly, he grinned, showing long teeth, yellow like Gandy's. "One advantage of a horse over a tractor is that a horse can have another horse. Our little mare, one we use for the trap, had twins a few days ago. Want to see them?"

The mare and her foals were in a corner of a field under the shade of a tree. She was pure white with a dark flash on her nose, and the foals were white, patched with brown. They had legs thin as pencils. One was suckling, the other stood sheltered under its mother's neck.

Tom had never seen such green grass. It stretched away from the gate, glistening in the morning sun. He whispered, "Am I allowed to walk on it?"

Great-Uncle Jack cleared his throat. "Well," he

said finally, "That field's had cows on it. And sheep. And horses. So I don't see what harm you could do. Mind you, I'd put geese on it, too, only Harriet Davies runs the poultry for all of us around here, all we keep is a few hens for the house." He cleared his throat again, frowning. Then he said, "A cow curls her tongue round the grass. She doesn't crop it close as a sheep will. A sheep nips it off with her teeth close to the ground. Like a horse. So you put the cows in the field first, then the sheep and the horses."

Tom said, "Don't they get wet and cold out in the open?"

Jack Jacobs stared at him.

Tom said, "I mean, when it rains . . ."

Jack Jacobs shook his head slowly with a look of bemused astonishment as if Tom was speaking some strange foreign language. He said, "We'll go and say good morning to Milly, then we'll look at the wheat. Another few days and it'll start to shed, so Ted's begun mowing this morning." He fished in his pocket and brought out a small, rough-looking apple. "Here," he said. "You give this to Milly. Open your hand so she don't bite your fingers."

Tom took a deep breath and thrust his hand forward, half-closing his eyes, and was surprised at the velvety feel of the mare's mouth and the delicate way she took the apple with her lips. He opened his eyes and patted her shining neck. One of the foals came behind him and butted him out of the way to get to its mother's teat. Jack Jacobs laughed. He said, "We'll get a rope halter on that one tomorrow."

He set off, back across the field, out of the gate, down the lane, through another gate—all at a pace Tom found hard to keep up with. He found the job he was expected to do when he reached the wheat-field even harder. Uncle Ted was mowing with a scythe, the long, curved bright blade flashing rhythmically in the sunlight. "We'll use the horse and the mower once the edges are done," Jack Jacobs said. "Meantime we'll pick up behind Ted and see how you shape up tying sheaves."

Watching Great-Uncle Jack, it looked easy enough. An armful of straw, the grain at one end, a handful of straw from the bundle tied round the armful, the ends twisted together and tucked under the tie. But Tom's first sheaf fell apart before he had tied the straw round it. "Eyes bigger than stomach," Jack Jacobs said. "Never take more than you can comfortably hug."

He stood over Tom, watching him narrowly. When Tom finally managed to tie his sheaf neatly, he expected praise. But Jack Jacobs only said, "Took your time, didn't you? If you go on at that rate, it'll be winter before we get the harvest in."

Tom hated him. And the harder he worked the harder he hated. The sweat ran down his forehead and into his eyes. His back ached, his arms ached, his legs ached. His neck ached. The straw cut his hands, the stubble jabbed at his ankles. But he went on working. Not because he was afraid of Jack Jacobs now—he was too angry—but because he was proud. He would rather die than give up! He would go on till he *dropped!* He didn't stop, even when he heard the children shouting in the field. He went on until Uncle Ted said, beside him, "Time to stop, boy. You've not done bad for an Insider!"

He took the sheaf from Tom's hands and gave him a foaming mug of cider. "Your Aunt Mary's home-brewed will lay the dust in your throat. And I daresay you won't say no to a bite."

Aunt Mary was there, smiling at him. She was holding a wooden trug in each arm full of bread and slices of cold bacon and shiny red apples. She said, "Lizzie, help Aunt Polly get the little ones settled while I see to this boy. Your great-uncle says he's fairly earned his lunch now. Lay a couple of those sheaves together, now, Thomas, you'll find they don't make a bad seat when you're weary."

"Run you ragged, did he?" Lizzie whispered, close to his ear. She sounded unexpectedly sympathetic. She even fixed a sort of spiky chair for him with the sheaves before she ran off and he was glad to sink down upon it. He took the bread and bacon Aunt Mary gave him and an apple for later. It didn't seem quite as substantial a midday meal as he had always been used to. Then he remembered he still had his breakfast bread and cheese in his pocket. It was probably a bit squashed and sweaty by now, not the kind of thing he'd look forward to in the ordinary way, but at the moment it seemed a special treat waiting for him.

The children were running round the mown edges of the field, a piece of bread and a slice of bacon in their hands; Lizzie, the fat twins and Joshua, the aunts, Uncle Ted, and Great-Uncle Jack had settled on the sheaves. No sign of Gandy. Tom said, asking no one in particular, "Where is my grandfather?"

Aunt Mary answered. "He's over the Bent Hill to see Mrs. Davies." She looked at Tom's face. "Oh, my dear," she said, "didn't he tell you?"

Tom's stomach was churning. How could Gandy do this to him? Dump him here, going off without a word, leaving him to be worked to death by Jack Jacobs? Misery made his head boom. Afraid he was going to cry, he buried his face in his mug of Aunt Mary's cider.

Jack Jacobs said, "He's only gone to pay his respects to an old sweetheart, lad. He'll surely be back before dark and he'll be proud when he hears the good report I'm going to give you. You've worked like a Trojan. Those were an ancient folk—I don't suppose you've heard of them, you have different sort of schooling on the other side of the Wall—but they were famous for working like you worked this morning. As if your life hung upon it."

He sounded so different, slave-driver turned kindly great-uncle, that Tom stared, his mouth hanging open. To his utter amazement, Jack Jacobs winked at him. "Well, you've done enough for the day, Trojan Thomas. If you like, you can take it easy, playing with the others, and chasing the rabbits."

To begin with, while the grown-ups followed behind the big carthorse that pulled the clattering mower, Tom and Lizzie played with the babies, galloping them round the field on their backs. Joshua gurgled damply into Tom's neck, tugging at his hair with fat little fists, and when he stopped to get his breath thumped him in the ribs with his heels to get him going again.

"You're a bully, you know that? A monster bully." Tom put Joshua down on a soft piece of grass by the hedge and tickled him in the ribs and the baby wriggled and laughed and began to turn purple.

"You'll get him overdone," Lizzie warned. "He needs his nap. He'll go off if you leave him now."

Tom stood up and Joshua started to yell, eyes screwed up and spurting tears, pink feet and hands flailing. Lizzie said, "Don't pity him, soon as you've gone he'll get over it."

Tom felt like a traitor. "Sorry Josh," he muttered under his breath. But Lizzie was right. When Tom tiptoed back a minute later, his eyes were closed, his thumb in his mouth, and he was peacefully sleeping.

For Tom, the rest of the afternoon passed like a dream. As the square of wheat grew smaller, the rabbits that had been hiding in the tall grain came racing out of the diminishing center, bellies stretched flat to the stubble, and everyone chased them with sticks. Tom almost hit one rabbit, but it got away; Lizzie caught another by falling on it and handing it, kicking and desperate, to Uncle Ted who twisted its neck until it hung limp and still. Tom felt sick, but excited, too. He said, to Lizzie, "It's horrible, really. Killing things."

"Mother makes a good rabbit pie," Lizzie said. "If you don't want it, there'll be more for the rest of us. But that's the last one, if it makes you feel better."

The field was all cut. Uncle Ted led the carthorse and mower away, jangling and creaking up the lane. Aunt Mary went round with her jug of home-brewed and they all stooked the wheat. This was easier work than binding and Tom was pleased to discover he was quicker than Lizzie at picking up the sheaves, banging their butts into the ground, and rubbing their heads together until they stood up. And he was happier still when Jack Jacobs said, suddenly appearing beside him, "That's right, Thomas-the-Trojan, six or eight sheaves make a stook. A sort of shed. Sturdy but open so the wind can blow through. If it rains they soon dry again." He clipped Tom across the back of his head, very lightly. "Get a bit of rest now," he said. "You've earned it."

Tom was so tired, he thought he could sleep standing up. And he was filthy dirty: covered in harvest dust and bits of straw—down the back of his neck, in his socks, in his hair. He saw Lizzie with one fat twin, Aunt Polly with the other. He went to look for Joshua but he was gone.

Aunt Mary had taken him, or one of the bigger children. A relief, in a way, although Tom had been looking forward to carrying him, warm and sleepy on his hip or his shoulder. Like a little brother . . .

He yawned as he walked up the lane some way after the others, wandering a little from side to side, tripping over his feet. The hedges smelled nice, some kind of herby smell. It would be lovely to lie down somewhere soft, somewhere dry, and sleep for a while . . .

Lizzie came flying out of the yard gate. She stared at Tom for a second and shouted over her shoulder, "Tom hasn't got him," and ran to Tom, her fists clenched as if she were going to strike him. "What have you done?" she wailed. "Where is he? Where's Joshua?"

Chapter 10

Something grayish and woolly . . .

"I did look out for him when we left the field," Aunt Polly said. "But then Lizzie said she was sure Tom had got him."

Aunt Polly looked as shocked and pale as a cheerful, round, rosy woman could manage to look. Aunt Mary was crying, shaking and quiet in a chair, and some of the younger children were pressed close against her, hugging her knees, trying to comfort her.

Lizzie looked unhappy and angry. "I was *sure* Tom was taking care of him. He put him down to sleep. Joshua likes Tom, you know what Joshua *is,* it's not everybody he'll go to . . ."

"They've picked the wrong infant this time," Aunt Polly said. "An angel as long as he's sleeping, but I pity those Dropouts once Joshua wakes up and finds he's not where he expected to be." The high color flooded back into Aunt Polly's cheeks and she began to laugh wildly.

Jack Jacobs said sharply, "That's enough, Poll. Control yourself, girl! Tom, when did you last see him?"

Tom shook his head. "I didn't. I mean, not after I put him down to sleep. I did go to look, but he wasn't there. I thought . . . well, I thought . . ."

His chest heaved and he felt he was choking.

"All right, boy," Jack Jacobs said. "You're not to blame anymore than the rest of us."

"He's not to blame *at all*, Grandfather," Lizzie said. "He didn't *know*. How could he know? No one told him!"

Jack Jacobs frowned darkly and, seeing that frown, Tom was fearful for Lizzie. Although it still seemed strange to him, he knew that in this world a child had to be brave to argue with a grown person, and he guessed that the older the grown-up, the braver you had to be.

But Jack Jacobs only said, "Right, then. Ted, you and I best be off. Mary, stop bawling, it won't bring your baby back. If my brother James comes back before dark you can tell him we've gone up the Stiper Stones, tell him the Devil's Chair. He'll remember. Don't say a word to Tess, there's no point upsetting her."

He made for the door. Tom darted in front of him. He said, "Can I come?"

Jack Jacobs looked startled. Tom said, "Oh, *please!* I could carry Joshua home when we find him. He liked it when I galloped him on my back. And I wouldn't be a nuisance. I could keep up all right." He remembered how he had worked binding the wheat sheaves. He said, "I could *make* myself keep up."

Jack Jacobs said gravely, "You'd be more useful here. You're a big, strong lad and it'll be a comfort to me and Ted to know you're around to help take care of things while we're gone." And he looked beyond Tom and signaled to Uncle Ted with a jerk of his head.

Aunt Polly said, "And isn't there just a chance Joshua has suddenly discovered what his legs and arms are *for?* No one's thought of that, have they? That he might just have crawled off, down in the ditch where no one would notice him. Why don't Tom and I go and search round the cornfield? While Mary gets the older ones to help her make supper?"

They were trying to distract him, Tom could see, both Great-Uncle Jack and his daughter. Did they really think he wouldn't notice? That all children were so easy to fool? He looked at Lizzie and she winked back, which made him feel slightly better.

"Is the Devil's Chair far away?" he asked Aunt Polly as they proceeded at a comfortable pace down the lane to the harvest field.

"Further than I'd care to go with the night coming down." Aunt Polly looked at him sideways and it seemed to Tom that her eyes, blue like Tess's, were brighter and sharper than he had noticed before.

She said, "There's an old Dropout lives by the Devil's Chair, one that your Great-Uncle Jack has had dealings with in the past. That's why it's best he and Ted go alone if we want Josh back safe and well."

She waited. It seemed to Tom she was waiting for him to say something.

He said, "Lizzie said to ask you if I wanted history. I don't know if the Dropouts are history."

They had reached the gate of the cornfield. Aunt Polly leaned on the top bar without opening it. The sun was low in the sky and it flamed in her red hair and dazzled Tom's eyes.

She said, "Everything is history, Tom. Your birthday's history. You and I standing here are history in the making."

He said, impatiently, "I don't want to know that sort of teacherly thing. What I need to know is, who are the Dropouts?"

She raised her eyebrows and he knew she

thought he had spoken rudely and roughly. He longed to tell her that where he came from, the way he had spoken had been unusually polite for a person his age speaking to someone of hers, but it didn't seem the right moment for explaining to a barbarian—even a barbarian aunt—that manners were different on the civilized Inside. So he mumbled, "I'm sorry."

She smiled faintly, forgiving him a little but reproaching him more. "I'll try and make it as simple as I can for you. There were two kinds of people who left the cities when the Wall went up. The first kind left of their own accord because they wanted a more independent kind of life, harder maybe, but more freedom, and the second kind were thrown out because they were no use, sick people, criminals."

She stopped. The sun was behind her; Tom saw her as a black silhouette with a flaming halo. She said, "The Dropouts are not all of the second sort, mind. Some of those who left on their own accord were just trolly-lolly boys, lazybones who thought it would be nice to give a hand with the harvest occasionally, but were better at getting their feet under the table and drinking and singing than doing a proper day's work. And when some of the criminals found there was nothing to steal except the food the homesteaders were growing, they preferred to turn honest and grow their own."

"Can you change the other way?" Tom asked, suddenly thinking of Charley. "I mean, can a homesteader turn into a Dropout?"

"It happens," Aunt Polly said, rather sternly, as if she guessed who Tom was talking about and didn't want to discuss it.

He said, "Lizzie said they'd got nastier lately. She didn't say how. I didn't think she meant the Dropouts went around kidnapping babies."

He though of Joshua, frightened and crying, surrounded by dark, hairy strangers, and a cold pit of fear seemed to open before him. He said, "They won't hurt him, will they? He'll come back, won't he?"

"Oh, surely," Aunt Polly said—a little too quickly and cheerfully for Tom to believe her. Then she went on, more convincingly, "It depends what they want, if we've got it. If we haven't, we should be able to get it. Food, drink, warm clothes against the winter that's coming. We've a good weaver this side Bishop's Castle. And it's not in their interests to ask for more than we can manage to give them. They learned that lesson when they set about burning the ricks. No bread for anyone that-a-way. Mind you, Tom, you can't depend on them seeing reason. Not those sort of ignorant people."

She gave a contemptuous sniff and pushed the gate open.

Tom said, "You don't really think he crawled away, do you?"

She didn't answer directly. She said, "Better to do something than nothing. Besides, Mary will get herself together better if I'm not there to take over." She set off down one side of the field, calling "Josh, hey Josh, if you can hear me, just whistle," glancing at the ditch now and then, but not seriously searching.

Tom went straight to the place where he had set the little boy down. He stared at the grass and said, under his breath, "I'm going to close my eyes and count ten and when I open them, everything will be as it was before. Joshua will be there, still quiet and sleeping."

He screwed his eyes shut and counted to ten and then another ten just to make sure. He opened his eyes very slowly and peeped through his lashes but although he had almost believed in it, the magic hadn't worked. The patch of grass was still empty. The ditch behind it was shallow, nothing but nettles, but there was a gap in the hedge on the other side that looked as if someone had pushed a way through it quite recently: broken branches, and a scatter of green leaves, freshly fallen.

He was down in the ditch in an instant, brushing the nettles away with his bare hands, looking for footprints. But the nettles had been growing too thickly and the earth under the hedge was packed dry. If thieves had stolen the baby while he was sleeping, they must have been quick and quiet to have escaped without being seen. Of course, everyone had been busy stooking the sheaves and catching the rabbits . . .

The hedge was thick. As the thief pushed through it, Joshua in his arms, something the baby was wearing might have caught on the brambles, the twiggy branches. Somewhere about man-height. Unless it had been an animal that had taken him! Some wild creature, dragging him on the ground! Lizzie had talked about foxes. They killed chickens. Joshua wasn't all that much larger than a big chicken!

Tom was trembling all over. Sweat was running down his forehead into his eyes, blurring his vision. He rubbed his eyes with the back of his hand but didn't really want to look, afraid of what he might see.

He heard Aunt Polly calling him. "Tom, give over, lad. There's no sign of him anywhere."

Tom's eyes were open now. He gazed into the hedge. What had the baby been wearing? Something light. Something that would show up in that dark hedge.

Then he saw it. Not high up, not man-height, but low down. Fox-height.

Tom lunged forward, scrabbling through the

rank nettles, stinging his hands; brambles scratched his face, tugged at his hair. He grabbed at it, at something grayish and woolly . . .

And stared, unbelieving. It didn't belong to a baby. It was a man's knitted cap.

Chapter II

It was Tess's secret . . .

He dropped it as if it had stung him. It wasn't until very much later that he realized what he had done.

By then he was standing naked in the copper, up to his knees in warm water. The copper was in a shed next to the pigsty. It was used for bathing people as well as washing clothes and when he got back to the house Aunt Mary had lit the fire in the copper hole and the water was steaming. She and Lizzie were bathing the younger ones in a tin bath in the kitchen but everyone else was to take a turn in the copper. Although Tom had not much cared for the idea of taking off all his clothes in an outhouse and climbing into a round tub with a fire lit beneath it, he did what he was told, partly because he was dirty and smelly from harvesting and there didn't seem any other way to get clean, and partly because Aunt Mary looked so red-eyed and solemn that it silenced any protest he might have made.

It was thinking of her sad face that brought it home to him. The woolly cap was important evidence of what had happened to Joshua. He should have given it to Aunt Polly straightaway. Why hadn't he? Why was he so *stupid?*

He danced his feet up and down on the bottom of the copper that was getting uncomfortably hot. A cooking pot rather than a bath. He supposed the idea was to speed up the turnover. No one would linger too long once they had started to cook! There was a tap at the bottom of the copper to let the hot water out and a tall metal churn full of cold water to re-fill the tub and cool the water down for the next person. This meant that everyone shared some of their bathwater which was something Tom preferred not to think about.

Fussy, he thought, as well as stupid! On the other hand, if he *had* produced the cap, he would have had to explain how and why he thought he knew who it belonged to. And that would have meant giving Tess away. He hadn't actually promised to say nothing about her night visitor, not in so many words, but they had been friendly together and she had trusted him.

He climbed out of the copper, pink as a boiled shrimp. He drained some of the hot water into a pail as Aunt Mary had shown him, and used a dipper to put in cold water from the churn. He threw his dirty clothes—Uncle Ted's dirty clothes—into a basket in the corner of the wash house and put on his own clothes that Aunt Mary had washed, his own trousers and underpants and the shirt Gandy had stolen.

He thought, *I wish Gandy were here.* Just to think it made him want Gandy more. Gandy would know what was the right thing to do. He could tell Gandy without being a traitor to Tess. Why had Gandy gone dashing off like that, without a word to him, just to see some old woman, some nasty old female barbarian he had known years ago! Aunt Mary had said he would be back before dark but it was *now* that he needed him. He could have jumped up and down with rage. It was so thoughtless of Gandy!

Lizzie was waiting outside the wash house. Her dark hair was tied on the top of her head; she was wrapped in a towel and carrying her clean clothes in a bundle under her arm.

"My turn," she said. And, with an evil grin, "I hope you didn't pee in the water."

"You are disgusting, you know that?" Tom said, passing on some of his anger with Gandy to Lizzie.

But he hadn't the energy for quarreling with her. He went on, more politely, "We don't talk about that sort of thing where I come from."

"Why not? You must have bladders on the Inside just like here. And all the rest of it. I mean, I *seen* you go to the privy."

"I know," Tom said. "Yes, it's silly. I'm silly. But if you must know, I didn't—well, you know what—in the water."

"Pee," she said. "Pee. It's a perfectly good word. Both the noun and the verb. I pee, you pee. Or pee, just pee, the liquid itself. Urine, if you're speaking poshly."

Tom said, "All right! Okay! You win! I'll *say* it. I didn't pee in the copper."

She was laughing now. He said, despairingly, "Lizzie, I don't know what to *do*."

He told her everything. Her owl's eyes grew even rounder and brighter. "I can't believe it! Grandmother hardly ever gets out of her bed!" Saying this made her laugh harder. She spluttered, "Except to *pee* I suppose! And the other thing!"

Listening to her laughing made Tom laugh too. But then he thought of Joshua, lonely and frightened.

He said, "Lizzie, I'll have to tell her what's happened. I'll have to go back to the field, get the cap, see if she recognizes it."

Lizzie's face was stern suddenly. No laughter now. She said, "Grandfather said Tess was not to be told. You were there, you heard him. *Everyone* does what Grandfather says."

"I don't have to!" He let out a huge sighing groan. "Oh, Lizzie, I do wish Gandy was here."

"What for? What can he do that you *can't* do, without him?" She was screwing up her little hooked nose as if she had a bad smell beneath it. "He can't decide for you, can he?"

It crossed Tom's mind that Lizzie didn't question *her* grandfather's right to decide what *she* was to do.

He put on a superior voice. "William, that's my father, says females are always illogical."

Lizzie didn't rise to this. Instead, the corners of her mouth started quivering. Tom said, couldn't help saying, "Where is *your* father?"

She hunched her shoulders and stared at the ground so that her face was hidden by a fall of dark hair. She said, very low, "He's dead. Last year. Last November."

Dead was a word Tom had never heard spoken aloud. Sometimes people said, *passed from among us,* but *dead* was like *brother* or *sister.* Or *pee.* But Tom was learning not to be shocked. The word *dead* was just another word that was not disgusting to a barbarian.

"Did he have an accident?" he asked, respectfully. He thought—*unless he was old!* But old people didn't have children, and Joshua was only a baby.

She shook her head, her hair flying. "He took sick with the fever. There were a lot caught the fever last winter. Old man Harris over the mountain. And two of the little ones in Aunt Polly's school died of it."

"*Children* . . . ?"

Tom couldn't believe it. Children didn't . . . He couldn't even frame the word in his mind. He said, stupidly, "Are you sure?"

"What d'you mean?" Lizzie glared at him now, her face white as chalk suddenly. "I saw their little coffins, didn't I? I saw them put in their graves. They couldn't bury them straightaway, the ground was too frozen hard. Nor my Dad, neither."

She ran into the wash house and slammed the door. Tom stood outside for a minute or so, wishing he could think of something to say. In the end, all he said was, "I really am sorry, Liz."

He knew it was feeble. She answered with a small choking sound, half sobbing, half laughing. "You don't have to be, it wasn't none of your doing!" And added, "You'd best go and tell Grandmother what's happened. It would just about finish my mother if something bad happened to Josh."

Chapter 12

Something he had never felt before . . .

Tess said, "I guessed something was up. That girl Mary, creeping in and out, looking like death warmed up—not that she ever looks *lively*—and lying in her teeth when I asked her if there was something amiss. Oh, no, Mother, what could be wrong, Mother, did you enjoy your supper, Mother, is there anything else I can get you, Mother, are you sure you are all right out of bed, Mother?"

Tess was sitting in a chair by the window. She was wearing a blue cotton dress and a necklace of blue beads and a blue ribbon in her hair. She looked very pretty: pink-cheeked and healthy. She slapped a hand hard on the arm of her chair. "What gets to me, young Tom, is the ingratitude of it! Night after night, I've worn myself out, staying up to all hours to steal a morsel of food for them, thinking of my poor Charley of course as well as bearing in mind that it might, along the way, keep us all a bit safer. You get my meaning, I hope? Taking my charity, those wretched Dropouts might have the decency to leave this homestead alone, take their thieving ways elsewhere. Instead, look what they do! Take my grandson hostage! As I said, it's the lack of appreciation that irks me! And on top of that, my own daughter not telling me the child's disappeared! As if I were nothing and nobody! Just an old woman to be shut up in her room and forgotten!"

She stopped to draw breath and Tom leaped in before she could start again. He was boiling with indignation.

"Aunt Mary kept quiet because Great-Uncle Jack said no one was to tell you what had happened to Joshua. He thought you might be upset. He was wrong about that, wasn't he? You don't care about anyone outside yourself. I've never seen anyone in my whole life so horribly selfish. You're lucky Aunt Mary brought you your supper and didn't throw it right into your face!"

Tom's heart was thumping hard and his ears were burning with anger.

"Lordy me, what a temper!" Tess's blue eyes were dancing. "No one's answered me back like that for a long time. Lizzie would like to; she enjoys speaking her mind, she takes after me in that way, but she's never quite got to the point. I suppose I ought to say thank you, young Tom! Nothing sets me up like a good quarrel. Gets the circulation going. Mind you, what my Jack would do to you if he'd heard you lambasting me, I don't care to think. Children should be seen and not heard is his view."

"Well it's different where I come from," Tom said sourly. "No one on the Inside would let a mean-minded Oldie like you get away with it. You've been spoiled rotten if you ask my opinion, everyone fussing and dancing attendance. When we had supper this evening, Aunt Mary saved all the best bits of the chicken for you. And she didn't ask any of us if we'd like a second helping . . ."

Tess hooted with laughter. "You've had rather too many second helpings in your life by the looks of you. Never mind, a night on the prowl will eat up the calories. You'll have to follow our friend after he picks up his goodies. He'll be off back to whatever cave or broken-down shack he hangs out in and with a teensy bit of luck you'll find Joshua there."

Mad, Tom thought. Doolally. Stark raving bonkers.

She went on, wagging her finger at him, frowning fiercely. "You go downstairs and say goodnight now; they'll think you're off to bed, but you'll come straight back here. We'll wait together till the time comes and all's clear."

He protested, "But Gandy's sharing my room! When he comes back and finds I'm not in my bed, he'll come looking."

"James won't be back tonight. Not if he's gone to see Harriet Davies." Tess winked at Tom and giggled.

He ignored the wink and the giggle. He said, "I've already said good night. I told Aunt Mary I was tired." He hesitated. Although he wanted to tell Tess what Jack Jacobs had said, he was afraid she might think he was boastful. He decided to risk it. "Great-Uncle Jack said I'd worked like a Trojan."

She nodded vaguely. She was thinking about something else. "I suppose Jack's gone after the poor little baby! And, you don't need to tell me, I know without asking that Ted's been fool enough to go with him! Leaving all of us here with no man to mind us; not a care for his daughters and grandchildren, let alone his poor, sickly wife . . ."

She picked up her skirt and dabbed her eyes with it.

"You're not sickly," Tom said. "And he said I could look after you. I'm big for my age and quite strong and not frightened. Nor is Lizzie." He thought about this for a moment. Then he said, "Do these people, these Dropouts, have guns?"

Tess shook her head. "Some of them did in the beginning, but the ammunition ran out and the brighter ones reckoned they'd be better off on the farms or learning a trade than fighting each other for nothing. They're mostly a feeble lot, nowadays. They're dying out, is what Jack says. They take a few sheep, a few chickens. Kidnapping kids is the worst thing they do. That's why Jack tries to keep ours indoors after dark . . ."

She stopped and listened, then put her finger to her lips and whispered, "Hide . . ."

Tom glanced at the bed, but the window was nearer and heavy curtains hung either side. He stood, pressed tight against the wooden frame, as the door opened.

Jack Jacobs said, "Not in bed yet, my darling?"

Boards creaked as he crossed the room. He was so close, Tom could have reached out and touched him. "Mary told me you were up and dressed when she brought you your supper. She's afraid you'll pay for it later."

He spoke very softly and gently. Quite unlike Great-Uncle Jack! Tess sounded different, too. She said, in what Tom thought was an exceptionally soppy voice, "My poor Jack. I've been such a trouble to you for so long. I've prayed for release but it hasn't been granted."

Great-Uncle Jack groaned. "Oh my darling . . ."

Tess made a strange noise, a kind of snort—as if she were trying to stop herself laughing. She said, sounding to Tom much more like herself, "I've decided to stop being a burden, Jack. Since I'm apparently not going to die, I shall make the best of a bad job and get up tomorrow. I don't suppose I'll be much use until I've got the strength back in my muscles but that shouldn't take long if I work at it."

Great-Uncle Jack was silent. Stunned, Tom imagined. Like Tess, he wanted to laugh. Until he heard her say, "Have you found Joshua?"

Tom clenched his fists tight, digging his nails into the palms of his hands. The curtains were brushing his nose. When he breathed, he breathed curtain dust. What would happen if he sneezed? Jack Jacobs would find out he'd told Tess. That he'd disobeyed him.

Tess said, "Now, don't look like that! I suppose you told them not to tell me and no one did. But you'd have to be deaf, dumb and blind! Deaf, anyway, and whatever's been wrong with me, I'm not hard of hearing. I heard the girls carrying on, so I did what I always do. I listened from the top of the stairs."

Jack Jacobs sighed—like a gale blowing. "No

one seems to know who took the child. No one we could find, that is. There was no one around up the Stiper Stones. And the only person we saw on the way was old Simon Watkins. He'll keep his eyes and ears open and pass the word to the Rangers. Ted and I will be off again at sun-up, soon as the horses are rested."

From behind the curtain, Tom heard his jaw crack as he yawned.

"Better get some rest then," Tess said in her new, crisp voice. "It's a nuisance this happening harvest time. At least I'll be another pair of hands. In the kitchen if not in the fields."

Jack Jacobs yawned again, hugely. "The boy's a hard worker. Looks a bit nesh but he's got a good spirit."

Behind the curtain, Tom blushed with pride.

Tess laughed. "Turning soft in your old age, are you Jack? Go on with you now. I can put myself to bed. And time you get back with Mary's youngest tomorrow, I'll be downstairs to greet you."

Tom was sure he was going to sneeze. *Hip, hip* . . . He wriggled his nose and pressed his bottom lip.

There was a creaking sound from the old leather of Jack Jacobs's breeches as he stood up. And the sound of his boots on the floor. And the bedroom door closing . . .

Tom sneezed. *Atishoo*. And stood trembling.

Tess twitched the curtain aside. "Good," she said. "I hope you heard all that. Don't get puffed up now."

"What's *nesh?*" Tom asked.

"Delicate. Not used to rough ways. Tender. It's an old Welsh word."

"What's Welsh?"

Tess rolled her eyes upwards. "Something from Wales. From the country of Wales. In Wales, you speak Welsh."

She looked at him and shook her head with mock sorrow. "Another time. This isn't a moment for education, I think. If I know Jack he'll be asleep in ten minutes. Ted likewise. If poor Mary can't sleep, Poll will be keeping her company in the back sitting room, out of earshot. I'll put up the bait for you in the dairy, and you take it out to the pump and wait for our visitor. There's plenty of cover to hide you and it's cloudy tonight so you won't show up in the moonlight. When he comes, he'll empty and trug. When he goes, you go after him. Quiet as a mouse."

Tom stared. *She meant it!* She really did expect him to do this crazy thing. Follow a Dropout to his home, like tracking a wild beast to its lair!

He ought to say no! It was foolish to go. And almost certainly perilous. His mother and father would never allow it. If Gandy were here, he would probably stop him.

"Okay," he said. "Okay, Tess."

He heard his own voice with amazement. He sounded calm as if he went around shadowing outlaw barbarians every day of his life! And as well as amazement he felt something new, something he had never felt before: a sudden, sharp stirring inside him, a strange mixture of fear and excitement. It was like electricity tingling through him, charging him up for something important, something thrilling and dangerous. It was a wonderful feeling. It made him feel ten feet tall and brave as a lion.

Chapter 13

"SORRY. C."

By the time he was settled in the shelter of the hedge he had shrunk to his normal height and felt about as brave as a rabbit. But the electricity was still running through him, and he felt sure he was ready for anything.

All the same, he was taken by surprise. He had looked away, or perhaps dozed off for a minute, because the night visitor was silently and suddenly *there*, crouching by the pump, taking the packets of food from the trug and packing them into a soft bag slung from one shoulder.

He packed swiftly and neatly, as if this was work he was used to. He didn't look round him; he had come here often enough to be confident no one would disturb him. He had long blond hair but no cap. Well, Tom knew where the cap was didn't he?

Tom's legs were cramped. He badly needed to stretch them. But he didn't move. He didn't take his eyes off the night visitor, who finished his packing and rose to his feet. He was very tall, very thin, narrow-faced with a long, bony jaw. He looked at the house once; a quick glance—perhaps checking the window where Tom had stood yesterday—then turned, and was gone.

Tom stood up cautiously, kicking his legs to get rid of the cramps, and followed the Dropout into the lane. He could see him clearly enough in spite of the clouds that were darkening the moon. And the blond hair gleamed pale in the shadows.

He walked fast, long-legged, loping strides; Tom had to run. Luckily the wind had sharpened, blowing the clouds into rags racing over the moon, and cracking the tops of the trees loudly enough to drown the thudding of a boy's running footsteps. Up to the top of a rise, then down into a ditch, through a hedge, across the corner of a field. There had been cows in this field, Tom, could smell them. He was wary of blundering into a sloppy and a stinky cow pat but he told himself this was no time to be fussy. The important thing was to keep up. And to stay out of sight.

They were into a wood now, which made stalking easier. When the night visitor stopped in a clearing, Tom hid behind an old oak, pressed against its thick, nubbly bark. He remembered how scared he had been of the trees when he had trailed Gandy through the Wild Wood, and could hardly believe it. He couldn't even think himself into the skin of the person who had had such ridiculous thoughts in his head such a short time ago.

The Dropout had settled himself on the ground, back against another tree—just a *tree,* neither a friend nor an enemy—and opened his food bag. He tore a chunk off a loaf of bread and stuffed it in his mouth, savaging it with his teeth, as if he were starving. Watching him made Tom feel hungry. He swallowed the spit that came into his mouth and although the Dropout could not have heard the tiny noise the swallow made, he looked in Tom's direction, frowning a little, as if something troubled him. Tom froze still, holding his breath, and after what seemed several hours the Dropout shook his head and stood up, swung his bag over his shoulder, and set off again.

His pace was steadier now, but Tom was tiring. He had worked hard in the harvest field and now his body was fiercely complaining, sudden stabs of pain in his back and his shoulders and his feet grown so heavy he could barely lift them. He gave himself orders. *One, two, one-two, pick your feet up, you can do it, you know you can do it . . .*

They had been out of the wood for some time now, trudging quite steeply uphill through some kind of low-growing, heathery plant that Tom began to feel would be lovely and soft to lie down on and sleep. He glanced up every few paces to make sure he could still see his quarry but he no longer cared if the Dropout looked back and saw him. He said to himself, *go on and get Joshua.*

The wind was wild now, howling across the open mountain. He had to lean into it to stay on his feet. Ahead, the Dropout leaped up the slope, light and quick as a goat. The moon came and went; the world was silver, then black. In one of its silvery moments, Tom looked up to see three great rocks on the ridge of the mountain. One of them looked like a chair.

The Dropout had vanished. Tom struggled on. He was hurting all over and each breath was painful. When he got to the ridge there was no sign of life on the other side of the mountain. Just miles of heather stretching away.

The wind blew into Tom's mouth, filling his chest. He spread out his arms to keep himself steady and shouted,

"Joshua, Joshua, JOSHUA. I want JOSHUA. JOSHUA. *JOSHUA.*"

The wind took his words and tossed them

around the sky. The tears spilled out of his eyes and ran down his face and ran saltily into his mouth.

He shouted with the last of his breath, "JOSHUA!"

But there was no one to hear him and no one to answer.

He turned back and staggered a little way down the mountain before his legs gave way beneath him and he crashed full length in the heather. It was both prickly and soft; it felt to him at that moment like the best bed in the world and, almost at once, he fell asleep in it.

And tumbled into a dream . . .

There were people standing beside him, laughing softly, and talking. He couldn't see anyone clearly, only shadows against the moonlight, but he could hear what they were saying. Most of it, anyway.

"Don't wake him, Dogger."

"No chance, he's asleep like the dead."

"Not surprising, all that good milk in his belly, scoffed the lot, didn't he? Anyways, not much left for the rest of us."

"Lucky to get any. Dang farmer near caught me. Came to take his cows in while I was still squirting away. Usen't to mind too much, that particular old fellow, didn't grudge a bit of milk now and then, but he's got himself a new dog, and New Dog takes a different view. A believer in Property. He'd have had my backside if I hadn't skedaddled sharpish."

"Serve you right if he'd bitten you, Dogger. You should never have poached from Jack Jacobs. I told you over and over."

"All right for you, Charley. Your Mam leaves stuff out for you. I need a coat for the winter."

"You can have my coat, Dogger. Put him down gently now. Don't want to wake the boy either."

Tom felt himself floating up, out of sleep, and then sinking. He was trying to slip back, into his dream, but the voices were fading and he was sleeping again, deeply and blackly.

He was cold and stiff when he woke. He looked blearily up and saw the three great rocks way above him, black against a yellow, dawn sky. Above him a bird was singing. And closer, beside him, something, some *live thing,* was snuffling.

Joshua's eyes were tight shut. He was chewing his knuckles. As Tom leaned above him, he opened his eyes and screeched with delight. He struggled to get his fat little arms out of the shawl that was wrapped tight around him. Tom picked him up and hugged him, and felt something crackle between them. He laid the baby down on the heather and found the piece of stiff paper stuffed inside the shawl with words written on it in capital letters.

TO MRS. TESS JACOBS.
SORRY. C.

Tom folded the paper with care and put it in his trouser pocket.

He said, "There you are, Joshua. She was right, wasn't she? Tess. Your grandmother. I think she's your grandmother, I get muddled with all these relations. Her name's Tess, and it was her son Charley hanging about as she thought it might be, collecting the food she put out. It was Charley some of the time, anyway. I don't think he can have stolen you; I don't think he'd do that, being one of your family. It must have been one of his gang, wearing the same sort of hat."

Talking to Joshua, Tom was trying to comfort himself. He felt very uneasy, exposed on the bare mountain with no trees or bushes to shelter them. Whoever had stolen Joshua, it was certainly Charley who had decided to give the baby back to his family. Where was Charley now? And the other Dropouts? There were no buildings anywhere he could see, no caves to hide in. All the same, he felt watching eyes all around him.

He said bravely, "It's all right, Joshua, I'm going to take you home now. You don't have to worry. Cousin Tom will look after you. Second cousin, really, I think, because Lizzie says she's my second cousin and she's your big sister, but second cousin is a bit of a mouthful, so I'll call you my cousin."

Joshua seemed to understand this. Certainly he appeared to be listening carefully. Then he gave a loud crow and seized a handful of Tom's hair and dragged it down to his mouth.

He sucked away eagerly. Tom said, "Are you hungry Josh? They gave you some milk, didn't they?" He thought—but that was a dream!

Joshua's mouth turned down at the corners and his face went red.

"Oh, don't cry," Tom said, horrified. What did babies eat and drink besides milk? He looked desperately round him as if he hoped to find bottles full of nice fresh milk growing on the low, heathery bushes. No milk—but some of the bushes were covered with small blueish berries. Tom tried one. It burst in his mouth, sweet and sharp at the same time. He popped one into Joshua's open mouth. Joshua mumbled it with his gums, considered, and beamed.

Tom propped him up on the heather while he gathered handfuls of berries. By the time he was bored with picking, most of Joshua's face and both of his hands were stained a rich purple color. It wouldn't come off—although Tom licked a corner of his shirt and rubbed away at Joshua's fat little cheeks and his stubby fingers, he couldn't shift it.

"Wait till Aunt Mary sees you!" he warned Joshua. As if he knew this was a joke, Joshua gurgled and waved his purple fists about, watching Tom's face intently, waiting for him to smile too. So trusting, Tom thought—which made him feel helpless.

An awful thought struck him. Even though he hadn't been able to find it last night, the Dropouts must have a hide-out somewhere on this mountain or Charley could not have disappeared so suddenly and completely. And though they had handed Joshua over, they might suddenly decide to take him back again. It could be a sort of cruel game they were playing . . .

With a queasy lurch of his stomach, he remembered one of the Oldies games he had played once or twice before Penny had stopped him. It was a teasing game for three children. The first would snatch something away from an Oldie, something like a stick that they needed to walk with, the second child would give it back, pretending to be ashamed of his friend's bad behavior, then a third child would snatch it away again. And all three would run away laughing.

Tom sat Joshua astride his hip and stumbled away down the mountain. If he could reach the wood he might not *be* safer but he would *feel* safer with the sheltering trees all around him.

But Joshua was heavier than he remembered. And, sensing Tom's fear, he began to wail and wriggle and stiffen until he became a very awkward bundle indeed. By the time they had reached the first trees, Tom had begun to feel he couldn't carry him another five minutes, let alone for the whole journey home!

He wondered how long it had taken to get to the mountain last night. He had been too keyed up, too excited and terrified, to look at his watch. An hour's march? Or two? And which way?

As he remembered it, the Dropout had led him straight through what had seemed then a fairly shallow wood, not much more than a band of trees at the bottom of the heathery mountain. But he had no one to follow now and the wood seemed bigger and denser in daylight than it had in the darkness.

He bounced Joshua on his hip and said, "What d'you reckon, Josh? This way, or that?"

Joshua seemed to have no opinion either way. He was hanging on to Tom's shirt, dribbling on it, his head drooping with sleep.

So Tom trudged on, hoping that if he kept his back to the mountain he would come through the wood eventually and land up in the field full of cow pats. Once there, he could probably find his way home.

The word *home* came into his head without his consciously thinking it.

He was on a narrow, wandering path. It seemed to be leading uphill which didn't seem quite right, but not absolutely wrong, either. And since it was an obvious path, it was likely to lead somewhere. With a bit of luck, out of the wood.

"We'll get home, Josh, don't you worry," he said, but Josh was peacefully sleeping, a damp weight on his hip bone.

Tom kept an eye on his watch. He had been walking for twenty minutes, then thirty. He was beginning to admit to himself that he had lost his way when the trees began to thin out. The path broadened and joined a wider track, rutted and muddy, that seemed to circle the mountain. And, as Tom stepped on to it, he heard the rattle and jingle of harness. The carrier cart came into view round the corner, and Simon Watkins, Postman and Tale-bearer, waved his whip round his head and cried out in his great voice, "I spy you, young Thomas Jacobs. What are you doing with that child?"

Chapter 14

"I can speak, you know. I'm not a parcel!"

Joshua woke, legs and arms jerking with terror, threw back his head, and screamed.

"Look what you've done, Mr. Watkins," Tom said. "You frightened him, shouting."

He rocked Joshua in his arms until he was snuffling and chewing his knuckles again, breaking off from time to time to give a pathetic cry, just in case Tom had forgotten that he was upset and hungry.

Tom said, indignantly, "I just rescued him, Mr. Watkins. The Dropouts stole him and I just got him back."

As soon as he had spoken, he knew this must sound a strange story. He couldn't make it sound more likely without explaining what Tess had been up to. He did his best. "The Dropouts stole him while we were all busy harvesting. The old uncles went looking but they didn't find him. Then I followed a Dropout and he gave Joshua back to me."

Simon Watkins boomed—and made Joshua jump like a fish in Tom's arms—"How come you're so well acquainted with that class of person, young laddie? Don't make a whole lot of sense to me. Here's a boy, been here forty-eight hours, knowing nothing, apparently able to treat with a Dropout all on the level, like a grown man. A grown man who's been a Ranger these twenty year. You're going to have a lot of explaining to do before you're very much older."

He laughed and his laughter echoed back from the trees and across the wide, sunny valley that fell away on the other side of the track.

"I don't have to explain anything at all to you," Tom said boldly. "I'll be waiting till I see Great-Uncle Jack Jacobs. He won't be best pleased if you hold me up arguing, 'stead of helping me take him home fast as I can."

Tom reminded himself to be more polite to this ancient Oldie. (It wasn't so difficult; he was getting quite good at politeness!) He said, "Great-Aunt Tess Jacobs told me you were a really *really* excellent Postman and Carrier."

He crossed his fingers and smiled very sweetly.

"Did she say that now?" Simon Watkins whistled through his beard, making bits of it fly out like thistledown. "That's a surprise, indeed it is. I didn't think she'd have a good word to say for me. Not since I told her I seen her boy up the mountain keeping company with that gang of thieves. That was a while ago, mind."

The Postman's black, bird eyes glittered. He added, "I had the notion Tess Jacobs kept herself to herself nowadays. Outside the family, no one's seen her in a long time. Mad, some say, that's why Jack Jacobs keeps her locked up."

"She's not locked up." Tom started to be angry and then stopped himself. He said, calmly and reasonably, "She's been ill. She's getting better now. Last night, she said she was going to get out of bed and come downstairs. Where are the gang of thieves you said Charley was with up the mountain?"

"Questions, questions!" Simon Watkins roared. "Ask, ask! Boy your age should have more respect for your seniors. I daresay, being an Illegal, you're ignorant of good manners. That lot, Charley's lot, that is, if he's still with them, mostly hang about near the Stiper Stones. Good place to come down on the valley like wolves on the fold. That's in summers. Winters, they get a bit of shelter in the old aircraft hangar on the Long Mynd. The Long Mountain."

"Aircraft?" Tom forgot he was not supposed to ask questions. "I didn't know anyone had airplanes any longer. I know they used to have them in the old days. They were dangerous, weren't they? Monorails are safer and faster. That's what they say. Go by Monorail. Swift and Sure."

Simon Watkins played with his beard. "Don't know what you're talking about. What they had up in that hangar were gliders. Sort of a sport it was, gliding. Silent. No engines. You flew in the air like a bird."

Tom looked at the sky and wondered what it would be like to be up there, swooping and sailing with the clouds and the wind. He breathed deeply and thought he could almost imagine it. Flying above this mountain, flying high above the wide valley, flying over the Wild Wood, over the Wall, over Urb Seven . . .

The Postman's bellow woke him out of his daydream. "You getting up behind me or not? All the same to me which you do but I've got to be getting on. Not past Owlbury Hall, not today, but I can lift you a fair piece of the way. Far as Harriet Davies on the Bent Hill. Hold tight to the little 'un and I'll give you a hand."

He was amazingly strong. He swung Tom and Joshua into the cart as if they weighed less than a couple of feathers. Joshua chuckled and tugged at his beard and Simon Watkins fished in his pocket and brought out a small rosy apple and held it up between his thumb and his forefinger. "Let go my beard and say please!"

He spoke in his thunderous voice and Tom expected Joshua to start screeching and squirming with terror. Instead he untangled his hand from the white fluffy beard and held it out for the apple. He was moving his mouth about, his tongue wobbling loose as if he were trying to think what to do with it. At last he said, "Peas," very clearly, and laughed with delight.

Tom said, "That's the first time he's spoken." He felt himself swelling with pride. He said, "His first word!"

He sat on a pile of sacks and held Joshua on his knee while he mumbled the apple. He said—softly, not wanting Simon Watkins to hear him—"Oh, you are clever, Joshua, so clever. 'Spose I take you back *talking!* Try and say Tom. Tuh-ah-mm. Go on."

Joshua took the apple out of his mouth and put his head back and smiled at Tom wetly. He said, "Uurrrh. Rrrhrre. Bbrrhe."

"Not *quite* right," Tom said. "A very interesting comment, but not my name. Never mind. Better luck next time. I don't know anything about babies, you see, but I think it's fairly unusual for a person your age to hold a *very* learned conversation. I shall have to wait for you to grow up before we can really talk to each other."

"Br Br Br," Joshua said contentedly. He waved his fists about and dropped his apple. Then he gave an enormous yawn, stuffed his knuckles in his mouth, and closed his eyes.

He slept the rest of the way to Bent Hill Farm. They turned a corner and saw it from a distance some time before they reached it, a long, low stone building, tucked under a fold in the mountain and with tall, dark pines growing around it.

"That'll be Missus," Simon Watkins said. "Her in the white apron in that field below the house. Out feeding the geese by the looks of it. That's a relief. Geese can be savage when they's hungry. Break your arm with a wing soon as look at you. Mrs. Davies swears they're wonderful guards. Better than any dog, she says. And she needs them, living here in this lonely place with just the old man for company. Poor old soul's good for nothing now except sitting in the sun."

Harriet Davies waved when she saw the cart, then turned and started up the green slope of the field toward the house. When they turned into the yard she was waiting for them. She was a short, skinny Oldie with a lined, smiling face that was brown as a nut, and a lot of strong, thick, gray hair, twisted and fastened on top of her head in a knot.

"What have you got for me, Simon?"

"Something you weren't expecting," the Postman said. "You look in the cart. Oh, don't you worry, I've got all the things you were wanting as well. Including a couple of books from the book exchange that you've been chasing me for."

She came to the side of the cart. She was so small she could barely peek over the side. She said, "Good Lord above. A boy and a baby."

"Correct," Simon Watkins said. "But whose boy? And whose baby?"

She looked at Tom, frowning. She said, "Oh, it can't be! I know James said he'd brought his grandson out with him, and this boy looks like him, *could* be James himself, years ago, but what's he doing with you, Simon Watkins? James had left him at Owlbury, that's what I understood."

"You could ask *me* who I am," Tom said. "I'm not one of Mr. Watkins's *parcels*. I can speak, you know, if I'm spoken to!"

Harriet Davies laughed. "Oh, your grandfather said you could stand up for yourself. Not used to taking a back seat, he said. But he didn't mention a baby."

"Joshua is my second cousin," Tom said, very proudly. "He'd been lost, and I found him."

"Followed one of them thieving Dropouts, and talked him into handing the little 'un over. Scared the kidnapper silly, I'd guess. Cheeky way he speaks to his elders and betters makes him a queer sort of boy. Like a dog dancing."

Simon Watkins climbed down from his driving seat and hitched up his breeches. "Any chance of a word with your father, Harriet? I wouldn't mind a glass while I'm at it."

"Father is in the kitchen. And there's beer, and there's cider. Help yourself, Simon." She turned back to the cart and held her arms out. "Shall I take the baby?"

"He might not like it," Tom warned her. "He's choosy. And I think he's probably hungry."

"Just while you get down from the cart," she said. "You might drop him."

Tom saw the sense of this. And although Joshua stirred when he was placed in a strange person's arms, he went back to sleep almost at once and didn't wake up again until a cup of warm, creamy milk was put to his lips. He showed off by putting his fat fingers round it and drinking it properly. Tom had milk too, and a big slice of bread with goose dripping which was like nothing he had ever tasted before. It had a kind of sweet tang to it that Harriet Davies said was fresh rosemary. "Your grandfather is particularly fond of my dripping," she said. "He'll be here by and by and right glad to see you."

She undressed Joshua and washed him and found an old tee shirt that she said was a bit big for him but would keep his toes warm. By the time she had finished, Joshua was asleep again. He slept until after Simon Watkins had gone; he was still asleep when Gandy came, riding into the yard on a carthorse, sandy and white, with a long, plaited tail. If he was surprised to see Tom, he didn't show it. He slid off the horse and kissed Harriet. He said something to her, speaking so low that Tom couldn't hear him. Then he perched Tom and Joshua up on the horse's warm neck, in front of the saddle, and mounted behind them.

"Well done," he said, to Tom, as the great horse moved off with a slow, rolling gait. "Tess told me what you were up to when I got back. That was very early this morning. I told her she'd gone out of her mind, sending a boy like you off on that sort of errand. But it seems she knew better than I did!"

"What d'you mean, *a boy like me?*"

Gandy chuckled. "You know what I mean, don't you, Tomkins? You've been used to a safe life. It was a lot to expect from you. It makes me proud that you managed it."

Tom leaned back against Gandy's chest. Joshua slept in his arms. He said, "Josh smells different since Harriet washed him." He yawned, his mind drifting. He said, "Have you ever seen an airplane, Gandy? I mean, a real one. Not just in VR."

"Airplanes? Flew overhead all the time when I was young. People went here, there, everywhere. Other countries."

"I don't understand about countries. Tess told me Wales is a country. They speak Welsh there. Great-Uncle Jack called me *nesh* and she said, that's a Welsh word."

Gandy was silent so long that Tom thought he had forgotten to answer him. Then he said, slowly, "Beyond the mountains, beyond the seas, there are other *places*. Countries, states, cities. Urbs, if you like. Or they were there before the airplanes stopped and the Wall went up. What there is now, I don't know."

"Doesn't Great-Uncle Jack know?"

"No, Tomkin," Gandy said. "Not even my brother Jack. He's got the world he wants all around him, why should he look further?"

"Are you going to stay with him? Or up at that farm with Harriet Davies?"

"That depends. More to the point, what do you want to do?"

"I don't know." This was too big a question, Tom thought. He said, "Mr. Watkins says I'm an Illegal."

Gandy said nothing. They had reached the lane to the Farm and he kicked his heels on the horse's side to make it break into a lumbering trot. He said, "Hang on to that infant now. Don't want to lose him in the last stretch."

The high hedges jogged past. Tom's bottom bumped up and down. Joshua woke and crowed and crowed with excitement. "Got a voice like old Watkins," Gandy gasped. "Wonder if his mother has heard him!"

She had heard him. She had been at the pump with her bucket. When they reached the gate she was swinging it open. The carthorse stopped and stood, its sides heaving. Tom cocked his leg over and slid to the ground. He said, "Here you are, Aunt Mary, I've brought you a present."

He put his second cousin in his mother's arms and felt lost at once. His own arms felt empty. Gandy, watching him, touched his shoulder and squeezed it, which made Tom's eyes fill. He wriggled and muttered, "Leave me alone, I'm all right," and ran to the barn. Behind the carts there was a ladder. He climbed it and found himself in a long, low loft that smelled sweetly of hay. He curled up in a corner and put his head on his knees and rocked backward and forward, to stop himself crying.

He thought of Joshua, safe home with his

mother and brothers and sisters and aunts and uncles and cousins and his grandmother and his grandfather. He thought of his own mother and father and it seemed impossible suddenly that they didn't know Lizzie and Joshua and the rest of the family. William and Penny were alone in their living unit, quite safe and comfortable, but perhaps they were missing him. He didn't think they would, but they might. Perhaps he ought to be missing them. But he wasn't.

He bit his lips until he tasted blood on his tongue. He lifted his head to wipe his mouth with the back of his hand and Lizzie was standing there, staring.

She said, "What are you doing? Everyone's waiting for you. How did you find him? Tess says she sent you chasing after some Dropout and Grandfather's furious with her. Well, only half furious. Mixed up. You know. Happy that Josh has come back. Angry in case something bad had happened to you."

"It didn't, though, did it?" Tom was suddenly smiling. "D'you know? Joshua spoke. He said a real word. He said, *peas*."

"Peas? Not carrots? Or turnips?"

"He meant, *please!*"

Lizzie lifted her eyebrows. "Amazing!"

"I thought it was," Tom said.

Lizzie wrinkled her nose. "Most babies start talking sometime or other unless they're deaf and dumb. What's amazing about it?"

"You've got loads of brothers and sisters," Tom said. "It's all right for you. He's my first one. Well, not a brother, though I wish he was, but it's all new to me. You're just spoiled. Moaning all the time, when *I* think you're lucky . . ."

"I'm the oldest," she said. "It's always Lizzie this, Lizzie that . . . stop those boys fighting, stop that baby crying, clean their silly faces, wipe their dirty and disgusting bottoms . . ."

"It's boring without them," Tom said. "I was bored before. I didn't *know* I was bored until I came here but that doesn't change it because I know *now*. It's not just having lots of relations, it's just that things *happen* here. Like—like, oh, getting the harvest in. And . . ."

"And babies being kidnapped? That was a lot of fun for my mother."

"*No,* you fool! I didn't mean that. It's just, where I come from, you know what's going to happen, not just tomorrow but every day of your life. Right up to your death day."

"If you don't like it, why don't you change it?"

Tom looked at Lizzie and saw she was simply asking a question, not arguing. He said, "I don't know."

She shrugged and pulled a face. "I wouldn't put up with it," she said, sounding like Tess, he thought. Then she giggled suddenly. "You've changed one thing around here. Grandmother is downstairs and driving everyone barmy. She's told Uncle Ted to get the old trap out so she can go visiting, and he's to make sure to polish the harness with mutton fat until he can see his face in it. And she's scooting round after Aunt Polly and Mother, complaining that nothing's been dusted or properly cleaned since she took to her bed all those years ago. Even Grandfather is getting to look a bit worried in case she starts finding fault with him somehow. It's made him less cross than he'd like to be about her and Charley."

Tom remembered the piece of paper he had in his pocket. He said, "She doesn't *know* it was Charley. I know it was, at least I know it was him gave Josh back to me, but she doesn't. Not yet."

He waited for Lizzie to ask him what he meant but she didn't. She only laughed and said, "Oh, Grandmother can be absolutely *certain* about something without really *knowing* it. She sent me to fetch you and if you don't come now, this minute, she'll *know* it's my fault not yours and I'll be in trouble. When she gets going she's worse than Grandfather."

And she turned and was gone down the ladder.

She called from the bottom, "Joshua has been crying for you!"

But when Tom ran into the kitchen, his second cousin was lying on his mother's lap, kicking his fat feet in the air and gurgling up at her. She looked at Tom and tried to speak but her eyes filled with tears. She shook her head and smiled, a shaky smile. He said, "He was very good, Aunt Mary. I think he thought it was an adventure."

Then he realized that the kitchen was crowded and everyone was watching him. He was horribly embarrassed. All the children, except the fat twins who sat in their high chairs and stared, began clapping. Aunt Polly seized hold of him without warning, squashed his face to her plump chest, and sighed. She was wearing a brooch with a very sharp pin. When she let him go, Great-Uncle Jack thumped him painfully between his shoulder blades and said, "Well done, Thomas. Though never go on that sort of dangerous errand without permission again! It was very wrong of your great-aunt to send you."

"She didn't send me," Tom said. "I *went*."

He heard a small sound and knew at once what it was. Tess Jacobs had a handkerchief to her face but he could see her shoulders tremble and knew she was laughing.

Tom looked up at Great-Uncle Jack. "It was my

fault he was kidnapped," he said. "I should have looked after him better. So it was my job to get him back."

He went to Tess Jacobs and stood at her knee. She took her handkerchief from her face and put her hands out to him but he didn't take them. Instead, he put a piece of paper into them.

She read Charley's message. She looked at Tom and touched the side of his face with great gentleness. She held the paper out to Jack Jacobs who came creaking across the kitchen to take it.

He read it and looked at his wife. "He won't have changed," he said, sounding heavy and sad. "A few years thieving and idling is unlikely to have given our Charley a taste for honest work."

"You could give him a chance, Jack," Tess said. "More of a chance than you gave him before."

"You think he'll come crawling back?"

"I think he'll come with his head high. But you'll have to fetch him," Tess said.

She looked at Jack Jacobs and he looked at her. Watching, Tom thought it was as if a quivering rope stretched taut between them. He had never seen grown people quarrel before, and his stomach clenched with excitement.

He found himself saying, "But Charley said he was sorry!"

Jack Jacobs swung his head round to face him.

Under his angry and astonished stare, Tom felt himself shrinking and shriveling to about the size of a beetle. Great-Uncle Jack said, coldly, "I will ignore your unmannerly interference this time, Thomas Jacobs. You have done us a service. But you will have to learn to control your impertinent tongue if you intend to stay with us."

"He may not be allowed to, I'm afraid."

Gandy stood in the open door of the kitchen and he looked hunched, and much smaller. Even his voice seemed to have dwindled; he sounded shaky and older.

He said, "The Rangers have come. They want to see Tom. And you as well, Jack. For sheltering an Illegal and trying to pass him off as your grand-son."

Chapter 15

Off the Road

"Out of the mouth of our very own Talebearer, I take it," Jack Jacobs said. "I'd hoped to stall him long enough to give me the chance of having a word with the Sheriff."

Tom longed to say Simon Watkins had known he was an Illegal long before Great-Uncle Jack had pretended he was his grandson, but he said nothing. He was too angry.

Gandy said, "I've shown them into Polly's school room. They want to see you and me, Jack. And Tom, of course. You don't have to be scared, lad. They won't eat you. Just you speak up, speak out, say what you want to say."

"He'll have no trouble with that advice," Jack Jacobs said drily. Then he winked at Tom as he had winked in the harvest field. He grinned broadly and Tom understood him now. Once he had shouted at you, it was over. Well, over until the next time, Tom thought and—rather to his own surprise—found himself grinning back.

They went through the back door of the kitchen, down the flagged hall, and through one of the heavy doors into the big room where Aunt Polly taught her school. There were small wooden desks with sloping lids, narrow wooden benches, and a blackboard—no Screen, no computers—but what startled Tom were the books. Shelves and shelves of them, reaching from the floor to the ceiling. He had never seen so many books in his life. And they didn't look like instruction manuals either. Although other kinds of books were not actually banned in the Urbs, they were frowned upon by the Protectors. "They put ideas in people's heads," the Chief Tutor had explained, calling the whole school together after he had confiscated a poetry book that had been discovered hidden in a boy's locker.

"Dangerous things, ideas," Gandy had said when Tom told him. Gandy had a few old story books that he kept under his bed in his room, in a suitcase, but Tom had never bothered to look at them. Now he looked at the shelves of books wonderingly. Lizzie had said she had read all the books in the house! Was it possible?

A loud, stern voice shouted "Boy," and he remembered where he was. The three Rangers sat behind a table on a raised platform in front of the blackboard. The one who had shouted was a fat barbarian with a pink, sweaty face—the first fat person he had seen on the Outside, Tom realized.

He reminded himself to be tactful. He said, "Sorry, sir. I was looking at the books."

The pink barbarian scowled.

Gandy said, quickly, "Not easily come by on the Inside. I was hoping he might have a chance to get educated while he was here."

"Was that why you brought him?"

This was another Ranger; younger-looking, and leaner than the pink, sweaty one, with a thatch of curly gray hair.

"He didn't bring me, I followed him," Tom said. "I thought he might hurt himself. I thought he didn't know what he was doing." He wondered how to explain this. Two of the Rangers were old, if not quite old enough to be Oldies. They might not care to be told that their brains were just about to wear out. He said, "It was a long time since he went to school. I thought he might have forgotten that the Wild Wood wasn't safe."

The third Ranger said, "Witches and warlocks and cannibal dogs? Giants and dragons? You seem a reasonably bright boy. Did you really believe all that nonsense?"

He had a smiling face and a coaxing voice. Tom felt more comfortable. "Not giants and dragons, sir. Just wild men, and wild animals." He decided not to mention the dangerous trees. He said, "I just wanted to take care of Gandy. Of my grand-father."

The third Ranger nodded. He looked at the notebook that was open before him and wrote something in it.

He said, "I suppose tales about ravening mon-sters lying in wait is one way to stop boys like you going wandering."

Tom said, "There's the Wall as well. It's electri-fied. That's what they tell us. And there are control towers all along. My grandfather will tell you. He used to be a Trusty."

"We know that," the fat, pink Ranger said. He sounded impatient. "Do you understand why your grandfather had to come here? Escape off the road?"

Tom nodded and looked at his feet.

"Well?"

Tom said, his voice husky suddenly, "I don't want to say."

He had told Lizzie, but to think of telling the Rangers now, in front of Gandy, made him feel faint and sick. He sighed and said, in his husky voice, "It's embarrassing."

The third Ranger, the nice Ranger, laughed. The second Ranger said, "*Embarrassing* doesn't seem a very adequate word."

"Awful, then," Tom said, through gritted teeth. "I mean, I know why. They keep telling us. There are too many people. So no one can have any brothers and sisters and when someone gets old and can't work anymore, they send him to the Memory Theme Park. And then—then he's got rid of. Like—like refuse disposal."

The tears came up in his throat, almost choking him. He turned to Gandy and flung himself against his chest. He sobbed, "Oh, I'm sorry. I'm sorry."

Gandy's arms held him tight. He heard Gandy say, "Did you have to force him to tell you?"

The Ranger with the coaxing voice answered him. "The boy has to understand the argument. You have an automatic right to asylum, James Jacobs, because of your age. But we cannot afford to take in large numbers of people who are not yet in your particular danger. It is a matter of keeping the balance. Occasionally we accept refugees who have special skills. We almost always send children back. We have enough of our own as you may have observed."

Jack Jacobs said, "This boy is a good boy. I'll

vouch for him. He's not a trolly-lolly boy. This lad'll work for his living."

"Is that why you claimed him, Jack Jacobs? To take the place of your own boy? Charley is his name, isn't it? Charley the Dropout?"

Tom turned his head to look at Great-Uncle Jack. He was sighing and shaking his head. He took out a handkerchief and wiped his face with it. Then he blew his nose fiercely. At last he said, "No one can take Charley's place. It's always here, waiting for him. I lied to that pest Simon Watkins for my brother's sake. He wanted to rescue his grandson."

"Simon Watkins is a useful pest," the pink-faced Ranger said. "Sharp eyes and ears and a wagging tongue. If we are to do our job, keeping out the Insiders, we need responsible citizens to act as informers. We can't just rely on nasty stories to frighten the children, and an inadequately electrified fence."

"I am a responsible citizen," Jack Jacobs said thickly.

The gentle-voiced Ranger leaned forward. "Let me explain, Mr. Jacobs. Think what would happen if we let in too many! They would swamp us. They would have to be fed. They would want jobs and land. Or they might join up with our Dropouts and become even more of a nuisance." He lowered his voice as if what he was about to say was the worst thing of all. "If they haven't already been sterilized, they will start to breed."

Tom listened, bewildered. He thought he must have misunderstood. He said, "But the Wall is to keep us all safe inside it. Not to keep us locked out . . ."

Suddenly they were all looking at him, the three Rangers, Gandy, and Great-Uncle Jack. No one said anything for what seemed a long time. Then the fat Ranger cleared his throat noisily. "That's what you're meant to think, boy. For your own good. What would be the point in knowing that you're on the wrong side of the fence? Ask your grandfather. Now I think you should leave us. Quick sharp now."

Tom looked at Gandy, then at Great-Uncle Jack. They both nodded.

It seemed a long walk to the door. The silence pressed all around him and made his ears hum. He went into the hall and out of the back door. There was no one about, no one to see him as he ran to the barn and up the ladder to the hay loft. He sat on the floor, hugging his knees and rocking backward and forward. He held Gandy's key, strung on its thong round his neck, and stroked it for comfort.

He wondered if anyone in Urb Seven knew what

he knew. William and Penny? He was sure they would have told him. His teachers? Gandy's father had been a school master. Gandy had said he had tried to tell the truth to the children he was teaching and had been "taken" by the Protectors. And that had been a long time ago. Perhaps nowadays there was no one Inside who knew, or remembered, or guessed, that their real rulers lived in the Wild. On the other side of the Wall. Perhaps it didn't matter. Perhaps they were all happier, being safe in the Urbs instead of Outside, where there was hard work and danger and children could die of a fever.

But they ought to *know* all the same.

He thought of his mother, and then of Aunt Mary and Joshua. Aunt Mary had Lizzie and Joshua and five other children. Penny, his mother, only had him. Was she missing him *seven times* more than Aunt Mary had been missing Joshua? In his mind he saw Penny with Aunt Mary's grieving face and it gave him an ache in his heart.

He heard voices outside. He crawled to the opening at the end of the loft and saw the three Rangers crossing the yard with Gandy and Great-Uncle Jack. They all seemed in high spirits. They shook hands and laughed noisily and slapped each other on the back before the Rangers mounted their horses, tethered to the yard gate. And when the men had gone, trotting down the lane, James and Jack Jacobs stood talking, heads close together. Then they both laughed and began strolling back to the house. As they passed the barn, Gandy looked up at the hay loft. "Come on down, Tomkin," he said. "Good news. You did well. Great-Uncle Jack did well, too. Persuaded them to make an exception. They will allow you to stay."

Tom felt his tongue grow thick in his mouth. He said, "I'm going back, Gandy."

Gandy shook his head, and put a hand behind one ear, as if he hadn't heard properly.

Tom said, "I'm sorry."

Gandy opened his mouth but his brother put a hand on his arm. He said, "Leave it, James." And, to Tom, "Don't rush it, boy. We'll be inside when you're ready. You just take your time."

Tom came down from the loft an hour later and walked to the house. He stood in the doorway of the big kitchen and saw Gandy, sitting alone by the fire. Gandy said, "Do you want to say why? Are you homesick for William and Penny?"

Tom said, "I'm homesick a bit, but only for them, not for home. It's just, they should *know*. Someone should tell them. Not just my mother and father. Everyone ought to know. For all sorts of reasons. People your age! And people like me who would like a brother or sister! But it's mostly the lies we've been told. They are all lies, aren't they?"

He watched Gandy nervously. Part of him wanted to hear he was wrong. But Gandy only sighed and said, "The Inside is a safe, sheltered place. A comfortable prison. The Protectors do their best within the limits set for them." Then he smiled at Tom. "Your parents will be glad to see you."

* * *

Tom stayed four more days. He helped with the rest of the harvest. He carried tiles up the ladder for Uncle Ted who was fixing the roof. He learned to milk a cow. He went with Gandy to the Bent Hill Farm and helped Harriet Davies weed her vegetable garden. He started reading a book called *Tom Sawyer* because the hero had the same name. He played with Joshua whenever the little boy was awake and told him stories when he had been given his bath in front of the fire in the evenings and was ready for bed. He sniffed him over and over again, so he would remember his smell.

Aunt Mary washed and mended the clothes he had arrived in. They were much looser on him than they had been when he came, and Lizzie lent him a belt to hold up his trousers. She handed it to him without saying a word, her owlish face screwed up and solemn. She wouldn't answer when he spoke to her. If he came into a room she went out of it.

The morning he left she was nowhere to be seen.

He hugged Joshua. He hugged Aunt Mary and Aunt Polly. He kissed Tess and she kissed him back, tears in her blue eyes, and said she would never forget him. He kissed the babies. He shook hands with the bigger children and with Uncle Ted and Great-Uncle Jack, who heaved him up behind Gandy on the big sandy carthorse. He felt the ache in his heart again. He wondered if it was going to break.

They didn't talk much on the journey. Tom thought he felt Gandy sigh several times. From time to time he said grandfatherly things like:

"Try and keep out of trouble."

"Be careful who you talk to."

"Even though everyone will listen, some people may not believe you."

"Be discreet. It'll be no help to anyone if you get taken."

They stopped around noon and sat on some rocks at the side of the road and ate the lunch Aunt Mary had put up for them: bread and cheese and pickles and several of what Gandy called "storm apples," small bruised fruit that had come off the trees in the wind. At one moment, when Gandy had disappeared into a clump of bushes, Tom thought he heard someone calling his name very softly. But when he stood up and looked round him, there was no one in sight. He decided it must have been the wind.

But it wasn't. When they came to the edge of the wood that bordered the Wall, Lizzie was there before them. She was sitting on a fallen tree trunk with her ankles crossed in front of her.

She said, "Hi, there! You've taken your time, Great-Uncle James, haven't you?"

She ignored Tom. He might not have existed. When Gandy slid off the horse, she went to him and put her arms round him and pressed her face against his chest.

She said, "Oh, Great-Uncle James! I'm so glad you're going to be there while I'm gone."

She looked at Tom then. She said, "You don't mind if I come along do you?"

Her clear, polished eyes shone at him. "It sounds my kind of place. Eggs already in boxes and no babies sniveling. And kids on top. Having the first and last word and all the in-between words. I'm not saying I'll stay all that long, mind."

Tom stared at Gandy. He said, "Did you *know?*"

"Let's say, I had an inkling," Gandy said. "I had a chat with Tess. You can guess she'd be all for it."

He tethered the horse to a tree and led them in single file through the wood. Tom had stalked Gandy through this dangerous forest. Now the trees were just trees, familiar and patient; the rustling leaves friendly. He wondered if he would ever be able to tell Lizzie how scared he had been. And why. Would she believe him?

He was terrified suddenly. If he couldn't make her believe him, how could he expect to make anyone listen? He was only a boy.

Except that they listened to children on the Inside. That was one huge difference between here and there . . .

They had reached the Wall. Just a sagging wire fence between one world and another.

Tom said, "Gandy . . ."

If only Gandy would tell him to stay! One day he might go back and fetch his mother and father. One day when he was several years older. And very much bolder . . .

Gandy said, "Lizzie should be quite safe for about another five weeks, I think. The Trusties don't run checks on children during school holidays. You can both come back when you want to. You've done it once, Tom. You can do it again."

In spite of his brave words, he looked at Tom longingly. Looking and looking, as if he wanted to hold him in his mind forever.

Tom said, "Oh, Gandy."

Gandy smiled. He said, as he turned away, "Off you go, both of you, under the wire. If you need help, Tom, either for you, or for Lizzie, or for your mother and father, remember my funny old friends and the Railway. And just you make sure you hang on to that key."